Caterin's Story
A Gift of Flowering Stone

Dan Erdman

be you
PRODUCTIONS
helping you enjoy life more

Published by
Be You Productions, LLC
www.BeYouProductions.com

ISBN: 978-0-9797426-3-7

Literary Fiction

Cover Design by Bonnie Schantz

Dedication: For my beautiful daughter, Catherine, who asked me to tell her a bedtime story.

With many thanks to Marifran & Ed Korb, & Marcia (Angel) Erdman, who encouraged me to publish this book, guided my hand along the way, and offered many hours of practical help. Thanks to Bonnie Schantz for the beautiful cover.

Thank you all for your wonderful friendship. It rises with the sun every day in my heart.

Contents

RAINBOW RING

"Oh my God! I can't believe this!" Our gnome-like professor appeared from behind a precipice on the narrow cliff ledge far above us. Along with my classmates, I peered up through the steamy sunlight after hearing the exuberance in Dr. Sitzer's typically sleepy voice. In a ceremonial gesture, he extended an object with obvious reverence and excitement. What he tried to show us gleamed and glittered through the jungle mist, as though he held the sun in his hands with a rainbow encircling it. Even from where we stood far below, I could see that his whole body was trembling.

"Can you see what it is, Diana?" asked Steve, who stood behind me.

"No, there's too much glare bouncing off whatever it is." Squinting up at the ledge, I called, "What have you got, Professor?" My voice ricocheted off the sheer rock face before us and seemed to dissipate in the circle of trees behind us.

Just before nightfall yesterday, Dr. Sitzer had noticed what appeared to be a shadow just above the ledge where he now stood. He had climbed up the rock face early this morning before the blazing sun had arisen above the trees to determine just what that shadow was. Now, obviously, he had found something, something

9

that transformed him from a book-wormish rock digger, into a shaking, screaming banshee.

"This is the most incredible artifact I have ever found! This is the most fantastic..." his voice quivered as he screamed back to answer. Whatever else he yelled dissolved into chaos as echoes swallowed it, leaving us dumbfounded.

"What is it? We can't see it!" I shouted. "It's too small, and the sun is glaring too brightly."

"Bring it down!" Steve added, and a chorus of voices joined in, anxiously encouraging the professor to return to the base of the cliff.

"Stay right there! I'm coming down! I'm coming down!" he responded with obvious delight in his thin, raspy voice. I could see him carefully wrapping the item in a red cloth, then slipping it slowly into his backpack. With less care than he wrapped the object, he clumsily rappelled down the cliff, as excited as a ten year old boy with a newly discovered lizard. I could hear him muttering during his entire trip down the slick face of the rock, but I couldn't make out a single word.

Finally, his feet touched down, slipping on the pebbles at the foot of the cliff as everyone ran to gather around him. "You just have to see this! And this is just a small part of it. I can't believe it...I can't believe it...I've never seen anything like this before!" he wheezed, out of breath from the exertion of his drop to our level, and his intense excitement. Slowly and carefully, he set his backpack against the foot of the cliff while we all crowded around to see this mysterious object.

"Stand back a minute, give me room...and..." With this, he stopped, stood up as tall as his little frame allowed, looked each of us in the eye with the seriousness of a semester exam, and whispered, "Don't you dare touch this or tell anyone about it until I tell you it's OK. Do you understand? This is my discovery...our discovery, and I don't want others crowding in on it." Shocked at this abrupt change in attitude, all of us fell back in silence, all except Grace, the quiet girl.

It was weird. As quiet as she was, Grace never acted timid. There was always a silent confidence, a hidden power about her, especially when we were hanging around Dr. Sitzer. Now, instead of backing up like the rest of us, Grace crouched down as though expecting the backpack to explode in her face, creeping forward to be as close as possible to the blast. At the same time, Professor Sitzer carefully wriggled the wrapped item out of his backpack. His hands shook slightly as he carefully unfolded the red cloth and allowed it to slip to the rocky ground, revealing the object.

Before the red cloth touched the ground, a lump had caught in my throat. Now exposed again to the sunlight and our eyes was the largest, most awesomely radiant piece of jewelry

11

I have ever seen. Dr. Sitzer held it with two trembling hands, as a hundred suns and a thousand rainbows seemed to shine, not as a reflection, but from within it. It was in the shape of a large ring forming an incomplete circle. As brilliantly as it gleamed, I was able to focus briefly on the surface instead of the light that reflected from it. I discovered that it was formed entirely of jagged crystals, with pyramid shaped tops pointing in all directions. It looked like a necklace, the open part to allow it to be slipped around the neck and hung from the shoulders. The underside, which would lie against the skin was smooth and clear as glass. But what amazed us all was that the crystals seem to have captured light in hundreds of colors, all as brilliant as the sun. As Dr. Sitzer trembled, the shining rainbow of color from the ring danced about. The light from within it was so bright that I had to keep looking away after brief glances.

We all stood for a moment as in a trance, staring blankly at the professor's find, all except Grace. Like a flash that beamed from the neck ring, she leapt toward Dr. Sitzer. With both hands outstretched, she snatched the ring from him before he had a chance to think of protecting it from her grasp.

"NO! NO! NO! NO!" screamed the professor even as she seized the ring. In one swift movement, Grace had grabbed the shining object from the professor's hands and slipped it onto her own neck. Dr. Sitzer stood aghast, completely overcome, in shock. He withered to the ground, his eyes intently focused on Grace.

Grace stood erect above him. What we witnessed next has been seared into my memory. The crystals of the ring emitted intensely brilliant light that flowed in tiny waves. The clear pyramids began extending like tiny glass fingers reaching outward, and simultaneously, the neck band expanded as though alive. The entire surface of the object stretched in pulses until it molded silently into one piece around the back of Grace's neck. Somebody screamed, and then others joined, unable to comprehend what they were seeing. Stephanie crumpled in a mass on the ground with a sigh, but no one moved to help her; everyone was frozen in shock.

But the ring was not finished with its metamorphosis. Tiny glittering vines spread like crystalline veins from the underside of the ring, stitching in and out of Grace's pale skin, spreading out to weave a tapestry on her shoulders and chest. Between the screams from our group, I could hear the tinkling of glass as the slightest of winds washed around us.

Finally, after what seemed like a very long time, the necklace stopped growing. Steve, usually a confident athlete, tumbled backward over the boulder on which he had been sitting. I could hear everyone gasp loudly together as they stared at Grace and the neck ring, which was still stitching threads of spider web-light over and under her skin. Ryan, the campus comedian,

13

always had a line for every occasion. Not now!
He fainted wordlessly and slid to the dusty earth.
The Professor held his hands over his eyes as
though he hoped that, when he uncovered them,
what had just happened would be undone. The
rest of us just stood gaping, unable to speak,
unable to move, barely able to breathe.

THE TOUCH OF THE RING

Before I had recovered enough to move again, I studied Grace, standing quietly before us all. She smiled, but not what I consider a normal smile. Not only did her mouth smile, but so did her eyes, her eyebrows, her forehead, her cheeks, her chin, her neck, and her hair. Her whole body smiled, if you can imagine such a thing! With the crystal neck ring on, her skin glowed, her eyes seemed to be filled with a gentle light, and her hands dropped to rest at her sides with the grace of a swan. Quiet Grace didn't seem so quiet, so reserved any more. There she stood, like a powerfully beautiful, living, smiling statue, a smiling statue in the middle of a steamy, sweating jungle, with a bunch of confused students, an unconscious clown, a stumbling athlete, and a bewildered professor. What a sight!

Grace opened her mouth as though to say something, but the only result was a stirring breeze blowing through the thick foliage from the direction of Lake Otho which lay beyond. This struck me as incredible since it was only the second time I had felt the air move since we arrived in the small village near the lake several weeks ago, the first being a few minutes before as the ring completed its metamorphosis. Grace opened her mouth again, and with another refreshing breeze and a rustling of moist leaves,

15

she quietly, yet confidently uttered her response to what had just occurred.

"I was drawn to the ring. I felt like it had called to me. Now that I wear it, I know it did call my name. I have never felt this happy in my entire life." As she spoke these words, she folded her hands together in front of her. When she did, a tiny white bird flew to the tips of her fingers, perched there for a brief moment, then flew above the professor, disappearing among boulders lying at the bottom of the cliff, the tiniest of white feathers drifting to the ground before us. I really thought that I couldn't take any more surprises like this, so I sat down on the nearest rock and put my head in my hands. As I did, I heard the professor talking to Grace.

"Grace, come here. Come, sit down. I need to know exactly what you are feeling and thinking. Just what is going on? I need to understand what is happening here." Then he called to me. "Diana, get your notebook... fast." At his words, I recovered enough to rush over to my pack in the shade of the nearby trees and pull out my notebook and several pencils. Meanwhile Dr. Sitzer was directing Grace to sit on one of the flat-topped boulders nearby.

"Grace," the professor repeated, "Tell me everything. Tell me what you are feeling, what you are thinking. How does that thing feel around your neck? Does it hurt? Is it tight? Did you feel it growing into your skin? Can you feel it under your skin now? What did you feel when it grew and closed? Can you move it at all?..."

As Dr. Sitzer spit out question after question, Grace raised an index finger and gently placed it on his lips and smiled, again. "Professor, I simply feel happy. I feel like a flower is growing in my heart and spreading all through my body. I can feel its beauty and softness...I feel like I know you very, very well...I know your dreams...your pain...your joys...your love. I see your future and your past, and I see in your heart right now." Grace paused, taking the professor's hands in her own. "Do you know that you have a beautiful heart, Professor? You have loved every one of your students with the heart of a father. And your own son...he understands why you left...he forgives you...he wants you to let go of the pain. She smiled again, and I watched as the professor sank back, as though thousands of rose petals had floated gently down on him, soothing any troubles he had ever felt. Grace kept smiling.

"Grace," I interrupted, "How do you know all this?" Since Dr. Sitzer's questions appeared to have gotten nowhere, I thought I would have a go of it.

"Diana, your heart has many questions too," Grace began as she touched the ring around her neck. "Many of the answers are within you, but if you want to know all the powers of this flowering stone, you must hear it from the voice of Caterin, in the high, secret place." With that, Grace pointed to the cliff ledge where Dr. Sitzer had stood just a short while ago.

"Wait," said Dr. Sitzer, recovering his scientific demeanor. "I saw quite a few items scattered around the ring in that cave up on the ledge...bundles and bundles of something wrapped in huge Paria leaves. The ring was sitting on one of them. Maybe we can find some answers there."

As he said this, everyone in the group stared at Grace. A moment later, a flood of questions broke loose among the students, each trying to understand what they had just seen. I guess each person was hoping, like I was, that others would say they saw the same thing happen; no one wanted to think they had gone crazily off the deep end.

Grace was talking with Dr. Sitzer in a strange combination of intense power and dreaminess in her voice as I stepped closer to her. Then she walked over to Steve, who was still lying on the ground, talking to him softly as she did. I got the sense that she was telling each one to whom she spoke little secrets of their hearts. After she left Steve, she approached me.

"Diana, you can stop hating yourself for the way you treated Thomas," she whispered to me. "His heart knows you love him deeply; that's all that matters. Let the rest go. There will be time to mend what was broken when you return to him." Once Grace said this, I found myself in her

18

arms, sobbing with relief, unable to understand how she knew of my heartaches. I don't remember telling her about Thomas, my crippled, drunken, drug addict of a brother. I don't remember telling her that I felt incredibly guilty because I had teased him mercilessly about walking with a horrible limp in his childhood. I certainly don't remember telling her I had grown to hate myself for what I had done, and what he had become. I couldn't have; I didn't recognize all the pain that lived hidden inside me until that moment. When she spoke those words to me, all the self-hatred and anger that I had shoved aside in my heart for so long poured out with my tears, falling from my reddened eyes, and melting away into the hard mountain earth. When I stopped crying, I felt light. I felt like a little kid again.

I wasn't the only one to whom Grace spoke such powerful words. In just a short while, she had reached every person in our group. I watched as she left individuals, smiling but tearful, just like me. Then, one by one, we gathered quietly, sitting down with sighs near the clump of trees under which we had eaten lunch earlier. No one talked about what Grace had spoken, but even without words, I could sense that each had been touched deeply by her kindness. There was a lightness in the air, a freshness, as though a cleansing rain had swept through with a brisk wind.

After some discussion, we decided, under Dr. Sitzer's guidance, that it would be best to wait until morning if all of us were going to attempt climbing up to the cave on the ledge to find the answers Grace had said were there. Since we were on the eastern side of Mt. Taree, the sunlight had already faded quickly from our campsite. Once we finished the plans for our ascent, Dr. Sitzer sat alone on a boulder in deep thought as the darkness spread all around us.

It was with much nervous giggling and more than a few spine shivers that we set to making dinner in the camp that night. Grace helped like she was a part of the group again, yet she seemed very different. She was somehow apart from the group, but in the center of us all. She flowed wherever she walked, and her hair appeared as though a light breeze was always blowing through it. Some of the group grew afraid of her, afraid of what had happened to her, afraid of what she might say or do next, afraid of what magic she might perform while they were asleep. I was curious, like I am sure Dr. Sitzer was, but I did not feel afraid. Grace acted strange; that was true, but I felt very safe in her presence.

After dinner and cleanup in the growing darkness and jungle night sounds, everyone settled into sleep, some more easily than others. In the middle of the night, I awoke to the noise of birds cawing in the distance. When I looked at Grace, silently resting in her sleeping bag, I saw her smiling face protruding. But the smile was not one of those pasted on types that people show when they are having their picture taken, but a deep, real smile. It was a smile that seemed as natural and real as her nose. The area of her skin around the neck ring still glowed, and the light shone all around, even on the underside of the huge leaves hanging far above her.

THE RING SPEAKS

I awoke to another moist morning, with the sun trying to pierce through the steamy droplets that arose from the jungle vegetation encircling the mountain. Grace and the professor were already up, sitting together under a giant oak tree, talking in hushed voices. The ring remained on Grace's neck illuminating her skin and the mantle of mist around her. Dr. Sitzer appeared entranced but in deep thought at the same time. As the others in our group arose from their sleeping bags, I noticed that most of them looked exhausted and haggard, like they hadn't slept well, if at all. Grace and Dr. Sitzer, however, looked fresh and energetic, eager for a day of adventure. I, too, felt terrific. Aside from waking once, I had slept soundly. I was anxious to discover what the day, the cave far above us, and the new Grace had in store for us.

After breakfast and cleanup, we gathered our gear and began to study the cliff's rock face to make certain that Dr. Sitzer's path up yesterday would be the best one for the remainder of the group today. Once we had finalized our plans, prepared our ropes and other climbing gear, and stashed our notebooks, cameras and food into our packs, we stood ready for Dr. Sitzer's OK to begin the climb.

After placing one last item into his backpack, the professor turned and stood to face the group. He spoke very forcefully about wanting to be the first to ascend the cliff, but with a calmly powerful voice, Grace was able to convince him that she should go, then he. The rest of us followed. When I arrived, I found both Dr. Sitzer and Grace carefully sifting through several bundles of Paria leaves which lay strewn about the floor. I watched as the rest of the students clambered into the safety of the cave. As Dr. Sitzer slapped his hands together as a gesture of finishing his task, some students were still removing notebooks and cameras from their backpacks. He waited patiently as each person shifted into a relatively comfortable position on one of the cave's boulders, then smiled calmly as he spoke to us. I could see that Grace's mood was beginning to rub off on him.

"Now folks. I don't have a clue as to what we saw occur with Grace yesterday, except to say that I know she is OK. I've checked her vital signs several times since I gathered my wits last night, and she appears to be functioning normally. However, this ring is not normal." He pointed to the crystalline ring, its light soothing the walls of stone around us. "I examined the vines running out from it which appear to have penetrated her skin. However, she didn't feel the vines growing, nor does she feel any pain from it now. I also examined the back of the ring where it joined together; I can't see a seam, a lock...nothing! When I tried to touch the vines, all I felt was Grace's skin. The neck ring itself is solid; that's for certain. As to why and how all this occurred, I just don't know. Grace has told me that we need to find the answers here, so that's what we're going to do now."

He shifted his weight and pointed around the cave as he spoke. "While you were climbing up, Grace and I looked around a bit here in the cave. Under that tongued shaped rock behind Frank, there were a number of bundles wrapped in Paria leaves. Well, Grace and I thoroughly searched these bundles this morning and discovered something quite interesting. Each of the bundles we opened had a group of thin wood slats with writing on them. I know a bit about the languages of the ancient people who lived in this area, but the inscriptions that we found on the slats of wood in the bundles are a bit more difficult for me to read. The words seem to be much older; it seems like these are root words for the languages I know. Sit down please before I continue." After yesterday, everyone was ready and willing to do this. Ryan, who had fainted and fallen, was wearing a rather nasty bruise on his face, and Steve had scratches and a thoroughly bruised ego.

It was Grace that resumed speaking after everyone was seated, before Dr. Sitzer could continue. "As he said, Dr. Sitzer and I looked over these inscriptions together this morning as you were climbing. As I looked at the first one, it appeared blurry. However, after a few minutes, the blurriness cleared, and I was able to read it as easily as if it was written in English. Dr. Sitzer was able to confirm that what I read was an exact translation as far as he could tell. I don't know why I am able to do this, but I am." She smiled broadly. No one moved a muscle as a cool, gentle breeze blew through the cave's dark recesses far behind Grace. I could feel goose bumps spreading down my arms and back.

Dr. Sitzer added his own comments. "It appears that these bundles all contain the same kind of thin slats of wood with generally the same kind of writing. They seem to have been numbered by the person who wrapped the wood slats in the Paria leaves and left them here..." He was going to explain further, but Grace interrupted with a quiet excitement in her voice.

"The explanation for the neck ring is part of what is written within these bundles; I know it is. As to what happened yesterday...I'm not really sure myself. When I saw the ring in Dr. Sitzer's hands, I had the thought that it was something that I felt naked without. Ever since I put it on, I have wanted to come here...to read what lies within these bundles...to help me find answers for myself...for all of us." She looked deeply at the Professor.

Dr. Sitzer continued again. "We searched around and finally found what, to us, would be the number one bundle. Then we tried to line up the bundles in the proper order so that we could read them as they were numbered. We've gotten that far. Before we try to remove these and some of the other items up here, I thought it best to have Grace read as much as possible to you while she can. I don't know why she can read these inscriptions, and for how long she will be able to do so, but we decided it was important to read it now. Once we have recorded it here, we can pack up the bundles and the neck ring, and send them with Grace to be studied in the lab back at the university. So, we plan to read as much of this as we can, right here. Once we have finished, we can start, CAREFULLY, MIND YOU, hauling it all down the cliff in the next few days. Under normal circumstances, I wouldn't let anybody open or touch anything this valuable before we got it in the lab, but my experience with Grace yesterday and today leads me to believe that these are not normal circumstances." He simply stopped talking then, and looked at Grace, as if she was to continue, and so she did.

"Dr. Sitzer wants to watch as I read so he can learn the words and phrases of this language. We will sit together here and I will read to you. Please tell me when you need to take a break." She paused and smiled at each of us. "After we found the first bundle, I discovered an inscription on a smaller slat of wood, lying on top of the others. I am going to read the small inscription to you first, then the contents of the bundles, beginning with the first one."

"Here's what the small inscription says: 'You have taken a journey. Your journey finds you here, where my journey begins, where it ends, and where it begins again. So we meet. From here, you and I travel together to a journey's end and to a new beginning.

Within these leaves you will find the words of life for my people, for your people. Any who accept the gifts of the flowering stone, will be keepers of the words of life. Their hearts will travel beyond Tarantee, beyond the Sun, beyond the mists of the Great Lake of Deep Waters, and into our sun times, our dark times, our life times. Our hearts will meet in that place. And the words planted here in my life time are to be planted again like seeds in your heart, bearing fruit as does the Azule tree, when seed has met the light.' "

As she read this, Grace gently stroked the crystalline surface of the neck ring. When she finished, she looked up and beyond us, out of the cave. I peered out too, seeing the expanse of trees, the edge of a great jungle on the opposite side of the huge lake some distance from the cliff. Then she continued, without looking down at the wood slat before her.

" 'My name is Caterin. This is the story of my Life Time, my child journey into the dark depths of the Great Family of Trees, and the vast lands beyond, where few except the Visitors dare to go. As I traveled to the home of Condly, so too, can you walk with me. But fear not. As I go into the earth, I go into my heart, and you with me.' " In the light of the cave, I could see that most of the group were still astounded and confused by all that had happened and by what

28

Grace had just read to them. But, there was an attitude of waiting, as though they all expected something wonderful, something magical, yet very real to happen.

After Grace spoke this last notation, she looked up and smiled. Then she bent over, reaching for the top slat of wood in the bundle before her, she said, "From the little I have read so far, these look like letters to someone from this woman named Caterin. I'm not sure to whom they are written, but I guess we'll find out. I'll start with the top one and read them to you."

BUNDLE 1

HELLO MY FRIEND

I have wanted to talk with you alone many sun times and dark times. I want to tell you what I see with my eyes. I want to tell you what I hear with my ears. Many sun times Mutee showed me the way of your listening, and the words that I must speak for you to hear. The fire in my hand burned each time as she taught me the way of your listening. Now that I have learned, the fire burns less, and only when I speak long with you. Now, too, I can talk with you alone, without Mutee's feathered hands to help. Now I can tell you all about my sun times and dark times and carry the words to you that Mutee says for me to share with you. I will return to speak with you again.

My Silent Friend,
I talk to you alone as Mutee says I must. I am Caterin. My mother saw who I am when first I came to this place under Tarantee. Mutee says I must tell you that first. She says you must know my name and know it means One who has seen the light of the One in which she walks. I do not understand why you need know this. Mutee says the growing flower will show me a little more with each passing, so I will know. I will wait. The wind of this sun time says we must

cover ourselves so he can breathe deeply with the waters of the lake to clean Tarantee. I seek the fires of my father's house to find the cover in my body. I will carry more words to you another sun time. I will return to speak with you again.

My Silent Friend,
My father does not know you. He never learned how to talk with you. His eyes tell me that he is afraid to do so. His words say that some dark time, I will walk into the earth because of your power. He does not want me to talk with you. That is why I talk with you while he is in his growing place, and I am alone. He does not see you as a friend, but I do. I am not afraid of your power because when I talk with you, my face turns up, and I feel rest inside.

The wind rested this sun time, and the sun planted singing in us and in the feathered Ones. The trees are beginning to sing too, with small green and white words upon their branches. Mutee says it won't be long before the singing will fill the mountain with many colors. It is hard to talk with you. I have many words to tell you, but my hand still feels the fire after saying so many words to you. Mutee says that the more I speak with you, the fire in my hand will grow smaller. I will return to speak with you again.

My Silent Friend,
Mutee says I am to talk to you for my people and for children yet waiting to come to this place

from within the thoughts of their mothers. She says she talks with a friend, just like you, as I do. Her wooden friend stays in Mutee's secret, high place protected within her mountain friend, Tarantee. I will keep you here, in my own hidden away place, beneath the tongue of Tarantee. I tell no one where you stay when we are not talking. Mutee says there will be a time when you can meet the people of the village. Not now. I have many words to tell you about my friend Mutee and the people of the village. Mutee says I will have much more to tell as my sun times pass. I will tell you more when the fire in my hand has quieted. I go now to rest my hand and play. I will return to speak with you again.

My Silent Friend,

The waters of the lake fall from the sky in this sun time and dark time. The wind is breathing deeply again, so the Little Ones stay near Tarantee. I helped Mutee with the Little Ones this time. I do not want to go to the growing place as my father does. My father walks to his growing place even when the lake falls from the sky. Every sun time, he pulls the jungle from his own growth and argues with the earth with his hands. He also hunts and brings the bodies of the feathered and furred Ones so that we might eat, he says. I cannot look into the faces of those whom I eat. Their eyes speak to me of their brothers and sisters, their parents, the blue sky, and the laughing streams.

Other parents stayed within this sun time, with their own Little Ones. When I played as a Little One, I had stayed in the village and talked with my mother and my brothers, who lived more sun times than me. They are all gone now. When my brothers could stand and work and hunt with my mother and my father, they also left our house to go talk to the earth with their hands in the growing place. They hunted with my father within the darkness of the Great Family of Trees away from the protection of Tarantee. But both of them and my mother have walked into the earth. My brother Deflic left through the mouth of an animal that hunted him, and my mother and brother, Dadock, from a deep fire within. Now in many of my sun times, I talk to Mutee, the Little Ones with few sun times, the Old and Broken Ones who are getting ready to move into the earth, and you. I will return to speak with you again.

My Silent Friend,
My father told me in the dark time that he must work hard to raise the growth we take in. He says that he must fight with the earth to make her give what we need. He wants me to begin to fight with the earth and argue with my hands all the sun times. He says after my child journey that I must stand by him and walk to the growing place too. He says I will not have to hunt like my brothers, but that I will have to make the furred and feathered Ones ready for us to take in after he returns from the Great Family of Trees.

My father spends all his sun times now in the growing place, or beyond the dark wall of trees. My mother used to go to the growing place, but she also stayed home some times. Her face was always downturned. My father is so heavy when he returns. He comes to our fire just after each dark time has begun. His arms and legs and eyes are heavy. He sleeps with a downturned face. That I have seen. I have asked him why he fights with the earth when we have plenty to eat and more that we give to the earth at the end of each passing cold time. He says with a quiet voice that I have listened to Mutee for too long. I want to see the time of my child journey, but I do not want to see the time after. I am afraid. I do not want to fight with the earth each sun time. I will return to speak with you again.

My Silent Friend,

Mutee, my friend with many sun times and growing streams in her face, lives near our house in a small hut. She works too, but not the same as my father does, and my mother did. It seems more like she is playing with the earth. Some sun times we gather what Mutee calls gifts to take in, from our friend Tarantee. Other sun times, she walks to her growing place, like my parents do, but she calls it her earth gift place. She walks there with music in her feet. She says that she and the earth love each other. We walked there in the last sun time. She talked to the trees and flowers with music in her voice as we passed. When we arrived at her growing place, her face turned up even more, and she

35

bent to kiss the earth. Then, she walked among the tiny green leaves in the dark black earth with the same music that she spoke, bending and scooping the earth as she did. Even when she pulled the jungle from among her own growth, she returned it to its family and spoke to it with feathered voice. "My little friend. I will take you back to share the kindness of the earth with your mother and your father." Then she bent over each small green sprout of her own new growth, and touched them with her feathered hands, talking ever with music in her voice. It almost seemed like the tiny plants grew taller with her touch.

I know that in the last warm times, the one before the white blanket came, the earth gave Mutee many food gifts. Much of what we gathered from the mountain side and Mutee's earth gift place we took to the Old and Broken Ones. Mutee shared some with me but took in little herself. Why is Mutee so different from my father? I will return to speak with you again.

My Silent Friend,
I have walked many sun times with a friendly sun and Mutee. Mutee and I spend many sun times playing with the Little Ones. Their parents are in the growing places or hunting in the Great Family of Trees beyond the Lake of Deep Waters. Mutee talks to the Little Ones about the gifts of their families, the village, the trees, Tarantee, the lake, the earth, and Condly, the Great Queen. When she speaks, it is like a game to the Little

Ones. It is like her words step alive from her mouth and dance in the sunlight.

In the warmth of this sun time, we played the fish game with the Little Ones in the laughing waters that feed the lake. The fish were flying among the rocks as the Little Ones tried to name and follow each that they had picked as their own. "That one is Little Stripes!" said Anjou, my mother's sister's son. "He is the fastest of them all."

"He is certainly one that likes to dance among his brothers and the rocks," said Mutee. "Look at how swiftly he swims." Anjou seemed to enjoy Mutee's words as much as watching Little Stripes. He laughed, and his upturned face peered into the waters, following the movements of the darting fish. Mutee took a seat close beside him. She too looked into the waters with Anjou for a long time, talking about his fish with him, and listening to him make up adventures that the fish had in strange and wonderful places. I watched all of this as I too helped with the Little Ones. Something in my heart jumped when I was able to see Mutee share such moments with the Little Ones. I wanted to do that too. Then I would remember what my father had told me. I would grow to his size, go on my child journey, and return to work as he did. I do not want this to happen.

Before I close my eyes this dark time, I say to all the powers of the earth, the twinkling stars, the sun, and the waters of the lake, and of

Condly, that I do not want to walk as my parents.
I want to walk as Mutee. I will return to speak
with you again.

My Friend,
I spoke to my father about Mutee and what
we do together. He doesn't hear any of it with
his heart. He does not know why Mutee loves
the earth and how she can live as she does,
playing with the Little Ones, and caring for the
Old Ones. He talked with me about other
Mingdas that he has known, some who cared for
him when he was a Little One, playing in the
fields, under the protection of Tarantee in the
laughing streams that fed the Lake.

"I remember Mantoo, a Mingda man, who
played with me while my parents walked to their
growing place," spoke my father. "We had many
happy sun times with him. He taught us much
about all that we saw and heard. I remember
the stories he told us, the stories of the Great
Family of Trees and the lands that lay beyond.
He told us stories of Condly, stories that I
believed as a child. But these were just stories of
a crazy man who liked to play with Little Ones.
Now I know there is no Condly, only Thretting."

"How do you know that?" I asked.

"Even though I did not go beyond the Great
Family of Trees in my child journey, I have seen
enough. I have heard the tales of those who
travel, those who have gone beyond the Trees
38

who are not Mingdas. They say that we must be careful to do as we must, for Thretting watches and waits to take us into the earth with her. It is she who took Mantoo. Mantoo had told us that it was his time to walk into the earth, but after he was gone, others told me that it was Thretting that had taken him away from us." He stopped for a moment, and looked into my eyes. "It is Thretting who took your mother and your brothers Deflic & Dadock, and my brother, Cob, Mutee's husband. I was not watching enough. Mutee did not watch enough." With this, my father turned away to look in the corner darkness of the room.

I waited a long time. Finally he turned his face back to me. "Why do the Mingdas live as they do, Father? They played with you. They play with us. I like being with Mutee. She gives me feelings that I want to keep. Why does she call her growing place a gift place instead?" My questions seemed to make my father heavier and heavier. Then he spoke to me, but with an answer that gave me feelings I did not like.

"Why doesn't Mutee take her place as we do in the working fields? I have been to her gift place and the gift places of other Mingda. It looks no different than our growing places. The sun shines the same and the lake waters fall the same. Why does her growth rise from the earth so easily? How can she spend her sun times as a child? Even after Yongsee, her Little One grew to our size and walked into the earth beyond the Great Family of Trees, she was like this. She does not carry heavy thoughts while we watch and wait for Thretting. Certainly her house is not as warm as ours, but she does not seem to care." I could see a little storm rising in my father's face as he said this. I don't know why. "My feelings do not..." He stopped as though his breath was caught in his words.

"It was Thretting too, who took poor Yongsee," my father turned to say, with heavy eyes. Yongsee was my brother Cob's favored Little One, first one to come from Mutee, his wife. Yongsee lived long before I came out of my own mother's thoughts. "Mutee says Yongsee is still on the earth playing beyond the Great Family of Trees, that she has heard from him, but this I cannot see in my thoughts. Thretting took him, as she took Cob and Deflic, your brother, in the shadows of the Great Family. It does not matter what the Visitors or Mutee says. They tell us stories that do not rise with the sun. Then Thretting can take us in a moment of story thoughts, not watching." His words lay heavy in my thoughts before I talked with you, my Friend. Now I am not sure of the way. I will talk with you again.

My Friend,
I have not spoken with you for many sun times. I have been talking much to my own thoughts and had no words to talk with you. I could find no words that filled the hole in my heart. I thought that maybe, I would find the answers as I played, as I visited and talked with

40

the Old Ones, but I did not. I don't know why Mutee's face is upturned most of the time when my father's is downturned. I think about her, why her face was so different from my father and so many of the other Grown Ones. I thought of the words of my father in the dark time. Did Thretting take Yongsee, Cob, my mother and brothers, like he said? Does Mutee play with us because she did not give up her child life, as I wish to do? Does she hold the stories of Condly as her thoughts when she should be watching for Thretting? Or does she have some secret that my father does not share? I will talk again with you.

My Friend Who Shares My Secrets,
The sun times of full blossom are here now, but my thoughts have not let go of the questions that grew there. Each time I tried to talk of these with my father, the questions grew stronger, and I could find less and less quiet in my heart. I decided to speak with Mutee about my thoughts. As we stepped through the shady brush of Tarantee, gathering nuts that were hidden from the heat of brother sun, I asked her.

"Mutee," I asked, "why is your face different from my father?" Mutee reached to the leaf covered ground, taking the gifts of nuts that sister tree had left there.

"What do you mean, my little Caterin?" As she rose from gathering the nuts, Mutee's face showed her not knowing of what I spoke.

41

"Why is it that your face is upturned when my father's face is not? And why do the streams in your face run from the sides of your eyes rather than across the top of your face like my father?" Mutee looked at me. I could feel her eyes reach into mine as I asked her these questions. Then, she looked up at the sun, gleaming through the tree tops above us. Finally, she pointed for me to sit with her on one of the fallen tree brothers.

"I know what you mean," Mutee replied as she touched my shoulder with her feathered hand, then stroked my cheek with the lightness of sister bird. "My Caterin, I believe it is time for you to hear the stories of the Old Ones and the mysteries that we Mingdas carry as flowering stones within our hearts." She looked closely into my eyes, as though she were searching for something within me. "But these words are like seeds that we throw not upon stony ground." She stood back, placed her hands upon my shoulders, and continued in a slow voice. "I can tell that your ears are ready to hear. I can see that your heart is ready to grow these words. Not all hearts have earth that is ready to grow the seeds of these words." She stopped for a moment and folded her hands together on her knees.

She smiled and continued. "From this sun time until the time you leave on your child journey, I will tell you a little of the secrets of the Mingdas each time we meet. But you must

42

know, these are not secrets that your father has not heard. They are called secrets because not all seeds that are planted grow to bear gifts in this life time. If the earth of your heart is not prepared for the seeds, the seed will lie asleep there until the sun and wind and rain, and all the loved ones of Condly, have done their work to make you ready." I did not understand her words, but I listened and my heart grew quiet in the listening.

As we continued to gather the gifts of the trees in the cool dampness, she told me that she would tell me the story of her face if I would speak it to only you for now, my Tree Friend. "There will be a time, after your child journey during which you can share the story with others," Mutee said. "Now, the word-seed must lie in the dark, warm earth of your heart to grow strong. When the word-seed has grown enough to break free of the earth, there will come a time when you may show it forth into the sunlight for the eyes of others whose hearts are ready to accept the seed. You will know when it is time to speak these words as they grow inside of you, like a Little One grows inside from the thoughts of its mother." She picked up a nut from the ground, and placed it in my hand. "Be the earth for the seed that I give to you, and a beautiful stone flower will grow from your heart." From that moment, Mutee began to teach me her secrets, and my heart was quiet with listening. I will speak again with you my friend.

All while Grace had read this, Doctor Sitzer sat on the rock next to her, listening and looking at all that she read, taking notes furiously as he did. The rest of our group appeared to be listening intently, sometimes with expressions of curiosity or confusion. I, too, did not understand all that Grace read, in part, because I did not understand some of the words and phrases. Also, I found my thoughts drifting from time to time, set to sea in my mind by some of the ideas that Grace read from this first bundle.

The group had all been settled into somewhat comfortable positions, but they stretched when they noticed that Grace had finished reading the first bundle. As I stood and stretched too, I heard murmurings of questions and theories bounce among the students, but I was anxious for Grace to pick up the next bundle at her feet to continue. When she did so, everyone resumed positions of concentrated listening.

BUNDLE 2

I WALK WITH MUTEE

My Wooden Friend,

I see Mutee every sun time now. It used to be that I played with her only while she was with all of us, the Little Ones. Now, together, she and I play with the Little Ones in the early sun mist and walk together during the high sun time to the Old and Broken Ones.

Mutee teaches me little secrets each sun time, to see things with her eyes that have been here under the protection and shade of Tarantee all my life time. I saw them as a child, but now a flower is growing in my heart by seeing them in the way that Mutee does. I remember when I was a Little One, running out of my parents' house each time the darkness left. I would run after my brothers or play with those of my own size. I noticed the sun mist, but only to chase after it as the wind breathed, running after it down the stream valley to the lake.

Now, with Mutee's eyes, I see it as a most beautiful gift from the Great Lake, a feeling of cool ahhh. After each sun time, when the sun closes its eyes, the Lake spreads its soft blanket over the mountain, the trees, and growing places. The blanket covers the earth during our closed eyetime. Before the sun has stretched, awakened completely, and thrown back the blanket of the Lake, the Little Ones are already running and hiding in the mist among the rocks of the stream, and between the houses of our village, playing games and searching for adventures. With Mutee's help, I see the sun mist as my friend, as I also see Tarantee, our brothers and sisters, the trees, the sun, the stars, and our gift-friend, the earth. Now, as I play with the Little Ones, jumping with them from rock to rock in the stream bed, I can see this new beauty, and still play as a child, as long as the questions do not fill my heart, pushing away the flower growing there.

In the time of the high sun, Mutee & I walk in the shade of the trees and our friend, Tarantee, with dancing steps around the Lake. The Old and Broken Ones greet us with upturned faces and thin arms, stretched to touch our faces. Mutee has visited them each sun time for many hot and cold times, to mend their bodies and hearts. Since they are too tired to go to a growing place, she also brings them many of her gifts from the earth. She also gathers gifts from the grown Ones in the village who are children of those Old Ones who have not gone into the earth. I watch her each sun time, as she touches the old woman Karama's wrinkled arms with feathered hands, as she lifts the food to the old man Parpa's mouth to feed him, to help Tomat lift his head to drink the juice of the flowering trees.

It was in this place, of the Old and Broken Ones, that Mutee told me about her face. It was, in our last sun time there, after Mutee helped Tomat make his way into the earth that she told me this secret. She and I had walked through the village of the Old Ones as I was learning the secret of touching with feathered hands. For a moment in between the houses, she stopped, looked at the top of Tarantee and said, "Tomat calls in need to our hearts. Listen carefully. We are here this sun time to help him prepare for his journey." When she spoke these words, I did not know that she meant the journey into the earth, but I found out soon after.

Without words from my lips, my heart and hands followed her into Tomat's small hut. He lay silent on his mat and lifted a finger as we entered. Mutee, stooped to greet him with the song for a Little One, and lifted his head, helping him to drink the fruit gift that stood beside him in the wooden cup. His face upturned when he saw and felt, knowing it was Mutee with him. "Caterin & I are here to help you prepare for your journey, Tomat. Caterin is learning the ways of the Mingdas before her child journey. You can help her too, as you take your journey into the earth."

He nodded, and with a breath of joy, said, "As you say, Mutee. I will take your feathered touches, and some light from your eyes with me as I go. I am ready to begin, if you will help me." She told me that as the Old Ones prepared to make the journey into the earth, they often requested the help of the Mingdas. Mutee explained the preparations of the journey to me as she helped Tomat move his body so that his head lay close to the door of his hut. He had entered this lifetime from his mother with his head first, so he would take his next journey head first also.

As Mutee quietly helped to adjust his body, Tomat told the story of his lifetime journey, beginning with the journey into this life from the thoughts of his mother. As Mutee began covering the windows of his hut, he told many stories of his lifetime, in words that were hard to understand because of the weakness of his breath. When he began talking about his 1st child journey, Mutee had finished closing all but the small door, where the light of the high sun hurried in. She sat on the ground next to him and held his hands with hers. I sat next to his head on the other side of his body from Mutee, watching him talk, and her listen. Their eyes made a road between them, with unspoken words traveling back and forth as he told his stories. Finally, he said with a clear voice, with the sweetness of a Little One, "And so I arrive here this sun time, ready to journey again, dear Mutee. The One calls to me; I want to go now."

As soon as he spoke those words, Dear Wooden Friend, his body shook, and a deep wind slowly streamed from his mouth, as the sun mist streams to the lake. When he did this, Mutee stood, walked to the door, singing a mother's song loudly, and began pulling away the sides of

48

it, making the opening larger and larger, allowing more and more light to dance inside the hut. As she did this, several of the Old Ones walked into the hut with a large gray-white blanket. Tomat lay perfectly still as they lay the blanket on the ground, placed him in it with feathered hands. They sang a game song of a Little One, carried him out the door, as Mutee continued to make the opening ever wider. I followed them outside and down to the bank of the Lake, where Mutee sat down on a fallen tree, her arms outstretched to accept Tomat's body, as though he were a new Little One. As the other Old Ones lay him in her arms, they stopped singing, and Mutee sang the song of a new mother, the one that each of our village mothers used to tell us that she had brought forth her thoughts to the world in the form of a new Little One.

Mutee opened the blanket so she could see Tomat's face. She touched her lips to his wrinkled head, saying, "Welcome, Little Tomat, to your new lifetime." I helped the others who had stood silently as we lifted Tomat's body onto the raft that was waiting in the water. Mutee asked me to come with her on the raft. I climbed aboard and sat next to Tomat's body which was still wrapped in the blanket. Mutee pushed the raft to the deeper waters, telling the waters where she wanted to go with the arm of a tree. I had never been allowed to go out on the Lake before so my heart wanted to jump and dance as I watched the waters underneath, and trees on the shore grow smaller as we moved away from them. I looked across at the far shore wondering what really lay beyond the Great Family of Trees that stood there. Then Mutee spoke to me.

"Now that we have passed from beneath the shade of our tree brothers, we can return Tomat to the earth, as he arrived." She motioned for me to pick up the side of the blanket opposite her, and lift the end with Tomat's feet, allowing his body to silently slip into the dark waters. Again, she sang the song of a new mother as she folded the blanket and we asked the raft to return to the bank and the waiting Old Ones, her face turned upward.

As we stepped from the raft, they all greeted Mutee with laughter and upturned faces, all reaching out to hold her in their arms, or touch her face, all as though she were a new mother. We returned with them to the center of the village of the Old Ones to eat some of the fruit and other gifts from the earth that were laid upon a table there.

After this gathering, Mutee and I walked along the bank of the great Lake of Deep Waters. Mutee told me that we had acted as Tomat's mother, bringing him into his new world. "His body was empty though. Before we had taken it out the door of his hut, his heart had flown to his new lifetime. What you and I and the other Old Ones did was to remind Tomat's heart as it flew, and to remind us, that going into the earth is the way to a different life time, not an end to life times. Do you understand, Little One?" I wondered why she called me Little One now, when I had grown so tall.

But still, I nodded, knowing that I could see in my thoughts some of what Mutee had told me. It was like seeing the shadow twins of the trees that lived in the waters along the bank of the Lake, without really being able to look up yet to see the trees themselves. Even so, behind my eyes, I saw my brother, Deflic walk into the woods, and then I saw him no more. In other sun times, I felt the fire that burned within my mother and other brother Dadock. It had melted them. My heart felt a hole in its middle when I wanted to play and run with them, I wanted to hear my mother's songs, and they were no longer there when I called their names. It was a hole that had never been filled, a hole that swallowed games that we had played together, songs that we had sung, so that I could never play them or sing them again.

"Mutee, I understand some of this. But tell me, how is it your face is ever upturned, even as you send your good friend, Tomat into the water to see him no more?"

"Caterin, it is because of the message that Condly gave my heart that my face is upturned." She stopped to turn her face upon me as she said this. Her eyes appeared as though they had lights within them as she continued. "There are words that I will tell you that others cannot hear. There is beauty in our place that others cannot see. Many cannot know Condly as she really is.

Many cannot hear the words of Condly. They see only Thretting. Their hearts cannot accept the seed of flowering stone that Condly would plant in their hearts. But there will come a time for every one of us, when the message of Condly will take root and grow. When I traveled over the Lake and through the Great Family of Trees on my child journey, Condly gave to me the gift of a flowering stone that fills my heart each moment that I look upon its beauty. I will tell you more as we prepare your heart for your child journey and accepting the seed of Condly's message, but you must make the journey yourself to accept the gift in person. This I cannot give to you." With that, Mutee's eyes reached again into mine, and for a moment, the hole in my heart felt Mutee's eyes resting there, warming it, making it smaller, filling it a bit with her light. Then she looked out over the waters of the Lake as the shadows grew and the sun mist began to gather once again to blanket the dark time. We walked home to our village in silence. That was what happened in the light of the last sun time, my friend. I will speak with you again, My Friend who does not leave.

When Grace stopped reading these words, she glanced up at us, breathing a deep sigh. As she did, Dr. Sitzer tried to help us all understand a bit about what we had just heard. "It appears that this culture treated death somewhat like a birth into a new life. The ritual that was described does sound similar to that of other ancient cultures, but it still sounded like much more of a joyful experience than others that I

52

have studied, especially the act of dying itself. I wonder why?"

"I am beginning to understand what has happened to me," Grace said, almost in a whisper. "Reading about this death, and why this person Mutee smiles all the time...it feels right inside."

"What do you mean, Grace?" I asked. What is it about that guy's death ritual that felt right to you? And what is it about this crazy woman who smiles all the time that you understand?"

"I guess I recognize the joy that Caterin talks about that feels right. And I don't think that Mutee is crazy. She couldn't be so clear about things if she were. As for the death, as I read about it, I could feel the happiness of everyone who helped when the old man died. I don't know why. It's like they really believed that he was going through a birth again; they weren't doing all that simply because they had been taught the ritual. It really meant something happy to them. There is always time for joy in our life, isn't there Dr. Sitzer?"

Dr. Sitzer arose and stepped to the opening of the cave as Grace was finishing. But he didn't answer her last question; caught up in his own thoughts, he continued. "These rituals, the death and dying, the initiation into adulthood through some test, it all sounds very familiar. Yet there is something very different here, something mystical that I can't quite place a finger on." I could see a dozen pairs of eyes watching him, waiting for him to explain it all, to present a theory that would make it all fit together. He stood with his back to us, almost as though he was really talking to just himself. "This flowering stone in the heart? The child journey that not everyone completes? And a death that seems like the welcoming of a newborn? I just don't get it." Finally, as though recognizing that Grace was still there after a long absence, he said, "Well, read on, will you please, Grace. I certainly hope that the rest of writings in these bundles can clear this up more." As he said this, the entire group turned its attention back to Grace, who gently picked up the contents of the next bundle after opening the leaves that covered it with great care and tenderness.

BUNDLE 3

THE HOLE IN MY HEART

My Friend Who Does Not Leave Me,

The words I spoke last to you from Mutee opened my thoughts of many dark times. I had never seen someone walk into the earth before I watched Tomat's journey. When Deflic, my brother with many hot and cold times, had traveled into the earth, he was hunting in the Great Family of Trees. My father said that they never brought him back home since it was so far away. My other brother, Dadock said that Deflic had become the food of furred Ones by the time they found him. That's why they did not bring him back. Then, when my Mother and Dadock himself were ready to walk into the earth, my father sent me to my mother's sister to play with those of my own size. I knew Dadock was leaving the last time I saw him. His face was red as the fruit of the Azule tree and his arms felt as though a fire was within, the fire that melted him. He looked into my eyes, and as he did, I felt the hole in my heart from Deflic's leaving grow larger, and Dadock fell into it. That's when my heart knew he would be gone when I returned. It was at the same time that my father did not let me see my mother, who also had a fire within. When I returned from the house of her sister, she was gone from our house. She too, fell into the

55

growing, dark hole in my heart and I never saw her again.

I still walk each sun time with Mutee. My thoughts tell me that she knows of the hole in my heart. She touches me with light, feathered hands, and shines her upturned face toward me whenever I am looking into the hole for my mother and my brothers, meeting me in that hole and walking out with me. She teaches me a little each sun time that we share. As we play with the Little Ones, she listens to them each moment, and so with the Old Ones. As we walk from the main village along the bank of the Lake to go to the village of the Old and Broken Ones, Mutee and I talk and laugh, and on the edges of my heart's hole, there is a warming glow. These times I remember as I lie with my thoughts in the dark, alone in the house of my father. It is strange that as the sun times grow colder and my father warms the house with the fires of our brother trees, it still feels colder here than in Mutee's small hut and little fire.

I talked with my father of Tomat's journey into the earth. He looked at me with eyes that showed me the holes in his own heart.

"I cannot stop you from this preparation for your child journey. It is, as it must be," he said, as his body became heavier along with the growing darkness outside. He warned that Thretting often visited the village of the Old and Broken Ones, and she must have visited with Tomat just before his journey. "They say that

Thretting always visits a person just before they go into the earth, but no one is around to see or catch her. Sometimes, they say, she walks the person into the earth in some hidden place, as she did with Deflic. Other times, she puts a fire into the person, as she did with your mother and Dadock, then leaves before anyone can stop her."

"Why must I be afraid?" I asked.

"You must be careful. Thretting could take you into the earth if she sees you in the village of the Old and Broken Ones. Then I would face each dark time alone." His eyes looked into mine, then quickly turned away. I knew then why the Grown Ones like my parents who worked in the growing places had built the Old Ones' village. They did not like Thretting visiting so close to them and to the Little Ones.

My father had spoken of Thretting all my life, but I did not think her to be real until my mother and brothers walked into the earth, and I never saw them again.

The Visitors of the Queen have come often from the other side of the Great Family of Trees. They have told us that they are sent to listen to our life stories to tell the Great Queen, to let her know who we are, but my father says she herself comes to our village without being seen. My father is afraid to say much to the Visitors because he is afraid of what the Visitors will tell Thretting.

Mutee and the other Mingdas here call the Great Queen Condly because she speaks words to their hearts that rise with the sun. What words are these? What words did Condly speak to my brothers, if she did at all?

Is Thretting real, or is Condly? A cloud was filling my thoughts as I saw first, Thretting standing behind my parents and brothers, then Condly, standing with Mutee and the other Mingdas. Thretting seemed so real to me when my father spoke of her, but Condly seemed just as real when I listened to Mutee. How could the Great Queen be so different? Whose thoughts could I hold as my own?

I was walking with Mutee to the village of the Old and Broken Ones this sun time. As I looked at the Great Trees beyond the Lake, behind Mutee, I asked her, "Why does my father fear Condly? Why does he call her Thretting, instead of Condly?"

"It is because he does not see Condly as she is. He sees in his closed eyes a person that only lives in his darkness, what he does not know. Because he cannot see Condly like he can see you or me, he fears her. Whatever he cannot see in the light of his heart, lives in his darkness. So it is with all of us."

"But I do not see Condly either."

"Yes, that is why you must complete your journey if you desire an upturned face and the
58

lightness within that lives with it. Condly can show you the flowering stone in your heart. I can only help you prepare for your journey to see her face to face."

"What will I see on my journey?" I asked. Mutee answered this question but her answer made more questions in my thoughts that I knew I must wait to ask.

"As I have told you before, if you are able to complete your child journey, you will see Condly and walk in her village. On your journey, as on each villager's child journey, you will see those things that live in your darkness and those that live in your lightness." Some of Mutee's words gave light to my thinking. I was beginning to understand why my father did not have an upturned face. He had told me that he had not completed his child journey. But what had happened to him along the way?

"Mutee, why didn't my father complete his journey?" We had reached the old tree that had been cut flat. Mutee sat on its dark surface and looked out over the misty waters of the lake.

"It is good that you ask many questions, Child." Mutee spoke these words very quietly. Her answer told me that she would give more light to my thoughts, but not as quickly as I wished. After a long time of looking to the lake and the shadows of the other world, Mutee continued. "I will tell you more when your heart is ready for those words. It is true with many

59

who start the journey, that often the darkness of fear fills the heart, stopping the child before the journey is complete. Your heart must be ready to throw off the darkness as you walk toward it. The child journey is one that everyone must take, but not all walk its path or complete it when they are your size. When the sun tells me, I will take you to one of the Old Ones who just completed his child journey. He will tell his story." Mutee placed her hands on her legs as though she needed to rest a moment. Then she arose, looked once more over the rising mists of the Great Lake of Deep Waters, and turned toward the place of the Old Ones. "Let us go, Caterin. The Old Ones call to my heart." That was all the answer she gave me dear Friend of Silent Listening. I will talk with you again.

Dear Friend Who Knows My Darkness & My Light,
"It is time you hear more." I had been waiting to hear Mutee say these words for many sun times. The light is growing weaker with each passing sun time, and the Wind is breathing heavier again. For many sun times, Mutee and I had been playing with the Little Ones in the early misty times, and walking to the village of the Old and Broken Ones when the sun would show his strength. I had been learning the way of the Mingdas, how to speak with a warm wind from my heart, and how to touch with feathered hands, but I wanted to know the secret of the Great Queen. Now, as we walked to the Village

of the Old Ones, she said it was time. My heart leapt at the sound of those words.

The hole in my heart had been filling with more question thoughts. At least they were making the emptiness of the hole go away for a while. But with the dark time and my alone, closed eye times, the power of the hole, the power of darkness returned. My heart and my feet had been wanting to start my child journey, to find the answers to my questions, or fill the hole in my heart, but Mutee has held me back, as she has said, to prepare the earth of my heart.

Mutee looked up to the sun over the tops of the Great Family of Trees. Just as a cool breath of wind passed us, she repeated what I wanted to hear.

"It is time you hear more." I spoke the words over and over in my thoughts as we walked along the bank of the Lake. I looked into Mutee's eyes to thank her. As always, her eyes were filled with a light that spilled wherever she looked; she looked at me. The streams from her eyes grew deeper, her lips opened more; her upturned face breathed a Little One's laughter. Then she grabbed my hand and pulled me along in a child's run to the village of the Old Ones.

As we ran toward the trees on the way to the village of the Old and Broken Ones, many words moved in my thoughts with every step. I thought about my father's words, that Condly may be just a story of someone' s thoughts, and that

Thretting is the real Queen. I thought of the Visitors, and what they tell us of Condly. I thought again of what my father told me when the Visitors had gone from our village, that it was foolishness to know that Condly would help. It was foolishness to give away one's best growth, and my father didn't have time to feed and mend the Old and Broken Ones--that was for the Mingdas to do. The Old and Broken Ones lived on the other side of a stream that fed the Lake, in a place where it was easy to wash and gather drink but away from the great numbers of our village. It was not an easy place to go to from our place. I thought of my father's downturned face, and Mutee's upturned face. I thought of my own face. Was it like my father's or like Mutee? I wondered what I was to learn next from Mutee. Would she answer all of my questions? Would she tell me when I could begin my child journey?

Mutee stopped before we entered the wall of trees that bordered the path to the village of the Old Ones.

"Caterin," she began. I want to tell you more of Condly." I could tell from her eyes that Mutee was looking far across the Lake, far beyond the Great Family of Trees on the other side, far into the land of Condly. She turned to me and held both of my hands, making a road between our hearts with her eyes.

"Caterin, when you meet Condly, this is what you will see. Condly is very old in her body, but her upturned face looks like that of a new child,

62

with streams of light flowing from it. Some say her body is made of feathers, so light is her touch upon the earth and upon them. When she speaks, her voice whispers like the wind that greets the new flowers, and her eyes shine into all that look upon her face. This fills the dark holes in their hearts with light. To any whom she speaks, their thoughts are filled with songs of Little Ones. When my heart had journeyed to the land of Condly, I saw all of this." Mutee stood quietly for a moment. A feathered One lighted on her shoulder and sang a song of the early mist time in her ear. Mutee held up her hand and the feathered One hopped to stand within her grasp.

The feathered One looked up into Mutee's face, then flew off, singing as it did. In Mutee's hand it left a small white feather, furry as a feathered One who had just found the world from within its mother.

Mutee offered the feather to me. "This is for you. It is time that you leave the nest of our village. We will make ready now for you to take wings to your thoughts." She looked up at the mists above Tarantee. "Yes, it is time for you to leave on your child journey." She tied the feather to my neck with a vine from a nearby tree, and, touching her lips to my head, said, "As I tie this feather to that which makes your heart and thoughts one, I tie my heart and thoughts to you. Your journey begins here and now, even though it will be many sun times before you go alone across the Lake and into the Great Family of

Trees. May the One who gives you, me, and Condly breath, help you fly to your heart."

We continued along the path through the wall of trees as Mutee talked to me of Condly, her words flowing now as the Lake that falls from the dark, mist gathered skies. As we walked down through the muddy stream and under the drooping arms of trees, Mutee told me what Condly knew of Mutee's own life times.

"She knew of my time as a Little One. She knew that my mother, like yours, had moved into the earth when I was a Little One with few sun times," continued Mutee. "Then, when I finally visited with her on my child journey, Condly reminded me that she had sent the Visitors with feathered hands and words of light for my father and for me when my mother had gone. Condly spoke with me about many of my sun times and dark times, reminding me of happenings long smoked by many dark firetimes. Condly said she knew all of this because my father spoke to the Visitors as the sun rises and gave way for me to talk to them also. The Visitors often stayed in my father's dwelling, warmed by my father's fire, fed by his growth, and even clothed for their travel. All this, Condly knew, and more." Mutee stopped, looking back at a spot on the waking sun's side of Tarantee, high above the village.

"It was at that time, the time of my visit, that Condly told me words of flowering stone for my times to come. Condly told me to open these words every sun time in my closed eye thoughts

64

to see her again. She told me that these words
would lead me to play with the Little Ones and
help the Broken and Old Ones to prepare for their
child journeys and their journeys into the earth, if
only I would plant the seeds when I returned.
Condly told me to wear these words back to my
village as living stones around my neck, flowering
stones that grew from within my heart. She gave
to me a small flowering stone that she said would
grow as the flower in my heart grows, a flower
that would not fall asleep or return to the earth
as our flowers here do. When the mists return to
the Lake again, I will show you my flower, up
there." With this, she pointed to the spot near
the head of Tarantee that she had gazed upon a
few minutes ago.

As we passed into the shade of the homes of
the Broken Ones, Mutee spoke again. "The
secrets of Condly are as close as Tarantee's feet,
but as far away as its head. One must walk the
path of flowers and feathers to reach there.
Condly and I will show you the way."

I had heard these last words before. My
father told me that the Visitors had spoken this to
him after my mother walked back into the earth,
and the Visitors had later spoken the words to my
father again so my ears could hear. But my
father said that it was magic that did not rise with
the sun. Now, more than ever, I wanted to start
my child journey to find out for myself. But
hadn't Mutee said that I had already begun? Still
I wanted to see the flower of stone that she held
in her secret spot in Tarantee; I wanted to go

alone across the Lake of Deep Waters and into the Great Family of Trees to see what lay beyond. As I returned with my thoughts to where my feet were taking me, we arrived in the village of the Old and Broken Ones.

We helped the man with broken legs, Kalfiet, to clean his hut and give him growth. As we did, I told Mutee that my father had often spoken of Thretting, and I had listened to the visitors speak of Condly, so I could not see either clearly. "When I close my eyes, I see more than Condly. Sometimes I see Thretting in mists and clouds. Sometimes I see Condly with my father's hands. When I see Condly, her face was always upturned. When I look upon Thretting, her face was always downturned, with fire beneath her skin. Sometimes they both stand in my thoughts, with a face that they share.

"I know of what you see in your thoughts, Caterin," Mutee said. "Until you see Condly for yourself, no person can see her for you. Even if you listened to the Visitors and no one else, you could still not see Condly as on a sun time with no mist, nor be able to hold her words. You must make the journey yourself, as each person must." Then Kalfiet raised his head from his mat and spoke to me.

"Little Caterin, come here, Dear One." He motioned with his thin hand for me to come and sit at his side. "I tried to make my child journey when I was your size, but I turned back. The earth of my heart was not ready to grow the seed

66

that the Mingdas had given me. There were many times in my life when I thought I would finish the journey, but each time, I turned back."

"Why?" I asked.

"Oh, there was a different reason each time, my Little One. Mostly, the poison of fear, planted by the darkness that Thretting had spread through my thoughts and into the earth of my heart. I was afraid that I would meet her, not Condly. I was afraid that I would go into the earth through the mouth of a great animal or lose my way and wander through the great unknown for all my sun and dark times. I did not want to go into the earth. I was afraid that I would never return to the land of my father and my mother, my brothers and sisters. Now when I look back, I see that these journeys, although not completed, were preparing the earth of my heart, loosening the hardness of the dark that lived there so that I could one sun time reach the place of my true heart. So I did, in this last time of new growth when the flowers say their first hello to the sun after the cold time. But, by this time I could not make the journey with my legs, so I asked to be carried to a spot to sit alone on the bank of the Great Lake of Deep Waters. There I sat and waited, looking into the stillness of the Other World until Condly came to me. She was the like the sun and the lake waters, and the beauty of the trees, all in her face. When she smiled at me, I felt as though feathered Ones had picked me up and carried me far above their homes in the tree tops. She told me so many things in that visit

67

with her that I am still finding them as I explore my heart and thoughts each sun time and each dark time. And she gave me this, this flowering stone, to grow as the words of her heart are growing in mine." At this, he reached under his mat and pulled out a clear, pointed stone of many colors, with a bright light and strange beauty, attached to a long thin vine. In the small wooden room under the shade of the great trees, it should have been dark. Instead, a bit of the sun was caught in the walls, thrown from Kalfiet's stone which warmed us with its light. Never had I seen any stone like this before, either in the laughing stream, the Lake, or along any of the paths near Tarantee. Never before had I seen a flowering stone that held the light of the sun within its body. Shortly after, Kalfiet returned it under his mat, and, with the warmth of its light, we continued our work.

After we left Kalfiet' s hut, Mutee and I walked silently along the Great Lake of Deep Waters. We stopped and sat under a twisted tree with needled leaves, looking into the Other World and resting together. Then Mutee spoke from out of her silence.

"Caterin, this you probably do not know, but, Condly sees you well in her thoughts. Your father told me many sun times ago that he wanted to keep you from Thretting, so he told the Visitors little about you, and even some things that did not happen. He said that this helped his face from becoming more downturned. But I have told the Visitors each time they come what I knew of you since you had spent many of your sun times with me. On their last stay here, the Visitors told me that Condly wants to see you some sun time, and she hopes that you want to see her."

"She really wants to see me?" I asked.

"Yes," Mutee said. "She knows that you are now preparing to visit her. She hopes you choose to finish your journey to her home." I felt my heart leap and dance when Mutee said this.

"There is more that you may not know. Both of your parents tried to journey to Condly several times since they were your size. Both of them turned back."

"I know that my father tried, but was it more than once? You say that my mother and father tried several times?"

"Yes," Mutee said. "Your father has started many times, but each journey, while passing through the Great Family, he was called away by friends to hunt. He chose each time to hunt with his friends instead of walking the journey alone. He told me that he found his heart struggling with itself whenever he stood alone. The seed that Mantoo gave him has not yet broken through the earth of his heart."

"What of my mother?" I asked, since I had not seen her or talked with her since my time as a Little One.

"She began several times as far as the Lake of Deep Waters, but could not place more than one foot on the raft to cross it. She told me that she did not go on because the stillness of the lake made bumps upon her arms, and made the air harder to catch with her mouth. Each time, she sat, watching the Great Family of Trees, and the still darkness of the Other World within the Lake for a long time before she turned back. She told me that her mother and father had said to her many times, that Thretting waited in the stillness of the Lake and the Deep of the Other World to take Little Ones into the earth. These words she held, and they grew in her heart as thorns so that she would not dare glide across the waters you and I have already sat upon. The seeds planted in her heart by Mantoo lay sleeping still."

"Even so," Mutee added, "This is what should be. Your mother and father will finally choose to visit Condly when the earth of their hearts is ready to grow the seed."

"But my mother has already gone into the earth. How can she take her journey now?"

"Who lies in the earth and how they travel once they are there is not of my knowing. There are words in my heart that tell me that each person, whether on the earth or in it, in some sun or dark time, walks to finish the journey. These words of flowering stone were planted by Condly when I looked into her face.

70

Mutee's words stayed in my thoughts as we sat under the comfort of our tree brother for a long time. Few words passed between us. I looked into the Lake, seeing the twins of the brother trees in the Other World. The white, gathered-mist twins passed over and under us with silence and calm. I closed my eyes and saw my parents, each starting to make the child journey, each stopping and returning to the village. I saw myself, stepping alone on the raft that I sat upon with Mutee and Tomat. I saw myself gliding across the waters and reaching the other shore. Then I saw Condly with Mutee's hands, waiting on the shore just before the giant trees, and my heart told my thoughts that my time to leave was almost here.

Mutee stood to go. Before she began to walk, she asked me, "Do you see, Child?"

I looked at Mutee and realized that she was talking about what I had just seen in my closed eyes. "Yes, Mutee, I see and I know. It is soon I must go?" Mutee nodded with upturned face, and a faint light flew from her eyes to land upon my lips.

"We will prepare you in the sun and dark times to come. I must show you my flowering stone, you must stand strong before the thought of walking into the earth, and you must tell your father. Then it will be your time to go from here."

"Yes, Mutee," I answered. I looked once more upon the silent lake but this time I saw a great white bird drifting close to the sunlit surface. It was heading for the far side of the lake, toward the shore of the Great Family of Trees. I felt as though I had become that bird. I grew bumps on my arms and my face upturned as I saw the other shore just before me in my thoughts.

"It is joy you feel, Child. It is the word-seed taking root in your heart. It is your way, the way to Condly." Mutee touched my shoulder with her feathered hand, speaking these words to me. We arose and ran hand in hand with dancing feet back to the village in the cool shadow of Tarantee. I will speak with you again, My Friend, who shares the words of my thoughts and of my heart.

Grace looked up at us as she finished reading from this bundle. Dr. Sitzer sighed deeply as he too, looked up and around the cave.

Steve shifted in his seat and spoke up. "Professor, I'm not sure I get what Grace is reading. Can you explain it a bit? I'm not catching all that she is reading and some of the wording is hard to understand."

"Well, Steve, I think I can explain some of it. However, I will have to study this quite a bit to understand it all myself. Since you asked, though, I will mention my impressions so far. It appears that this might be a journal or diary of

72

this young person Caterin from a village of people that lived here next to Mt. Taree long ago," Dr. Sitzer answered. "I thought at first that this girl, Caterin must be preparing for adulthood. As many of you know, most civilizations have a set of rituals for initiation into adulthood. However, it seems like this child journey she mentions might be something different from that since it sounds like some adults, like Caterin's parents, have not completed it, and Kalfiet, the old man, completes it very late in life. Caterin appears to be preparing for this journey, but I am not certain exactly what she has to do and why. I am also curious about Condly and Thretting. It almost sounds like there is one person who has two personalities, and thus two names. Of course, this could be a mythical or religious character that doesn't really exist at all. We may find more as we read on.

There were some other things mentioned that aroused my curiosity quite a bit. Since there is some mention of the land of Condly, I wonder if we could find any evidence for its existence as well as artifacts that help explain more about Caterin's civilization. It sounds like it is east of here, beyond the lake and forest over that way." Dr. Sitzer pointed in the direction of the huge lake nearby, but continued with his explanation.

"The other very interesting item that I noted was that there is at least one other neck ring and more writings mentioned. It sounds like there is yet another hidden cave higher on the mountainside where this person Mutee kept her

73

things. If we search the mountain carefully, we might be able to find the other ring and her writings as well! He paused and took a breath, smiling broadly as he did.

I also want to let you know that I am learning quite a bit from following what Grace is reading. I know that some of the words and phrases might be difficult for you to understand, but they will become clearer as she continues to use them. Listen carefully and I am sure you will be able to pick up on much of the meaning." With that said, he turned his attention back to Grace who had already picked up the next bundle of slats.

"Is everyone ready to continue?" she asked as she glanced around the cave at everyone. "If so, I will read on." Everyone nodded their assent, so Grace began reading again.

BUNDLE 4

TASKS ON THE PATH

My Friend who walks with me on my journey,
The cold times are passing by as I prepare for my journey to Condly. I have had much to do, and with Mutee's help, I am able to do it well. It was a few sun times after our talk at the lake that she told me all that I must do. By that time the dark times were longer, and the wind was breathing cool. The people of the village were eating more and working less. The fires of the dark times were warming the houses for longer and eating more of our brother trees. When she was ready to tell me, we sat in Mutee's house, away from the cooler winds that had traveled from the other side of Tarantee.

"These tasks I give to you are your tasks; they are for no other. Make certain that you write this upon your Wooden Friend so if another catches your voice from her, she will know that each must have tasks from her own closed eye times." This Mutee said with eyes that spoke of its importance. I took the words from her mouth and placed them in your care, Dear Friend. I ask you to hold them for me and for others who might read them in some other time, as Mutee has told me.

This is what Mutee told me I must do.

75

"Child, you must first find a place in your closed eyes for Condly. You might have her there now as Condly, or Thretting, so you must prepare an empty place so that Condly is not captive in your closed eyes as someone she is not. With this I will help you by showing you my flowering stone and the words of my visit to Condly. You may also sit in my place within Tarantee until you have created this place in your heart for Condly." She placed her feathered hands over my eyes and closed them, holding my head as she did. "This place in your thoughts must stay empty until you see Condly face to face. Then you will have room for her. Also, before you walk to her, you must see the darkness under the earth, and to it, bring your own light."

"I do not understand this, Mutee."

"It will be given to you within a few sun times. Then you will know with no mists in your thoughts. If you can bring your light under the earth, you will be ready for the final step before your journey alone."

"What is that final step?"

"You must tell your father. He will be partly knowing that it is time. Still, a fire will burn in his heart for your leaving. You must face that fire without fear, and instead of burning in it, be warmed by the light thoughts that created it. Then, and finally then, will you walk alone to the raft, drift across the Waters of the Lake and the

Other World, and greet the Great Family of Trees."

I did not fully know in my thoughts what Mutee told me with these words, but I will close my eyes with her hands holding my thoughts and heart. I will speak with you again, my Friend.

My Friend,
It has been many sun times since I last spoke with you. I thought my journey would begin soon after Mutee had spoken of the tasks I must do. She said that the time must be right in the earth of my heart for each of these. In the light of the last sun time, in the early mist, I completed my first task. This is what happened. Mutee and I had gone with the Little Ones, as we do each sun time, to play among the tree brothers and the stream that feeds the Lake of Deep Waters. We were playing the game of rock jump, to leap from one to another in the midst of the waters that danced under our feet. This sun time, we played near the Lake, where the stream has waters that run deep, so dark and smooth that I can see the Other World clearly. Anjou, my favored Little One, the fastest, was far ahead in jumping the rocks. I was behind him, with the mists floating between us. I turned and looked behind to see the rest of the Little Ones following with Mutee. As I did, I saw her point in the direction that Anjou had been running ahead of me as she called to me.

"Anjou has slipped into the Other World," Mutee said in a voice that was louder than the voice of the stream. "You must find him and bring him back. It is not his time to go into the earth." At her words, I turned around to see where Anjou had been, seeing only circles on the water. Anjou had disappeared into the darkness of the Deep Waters.

I took one more look at Tarantee before I pointed and threw my body toward the middle of the circle, into the darkness. When I entered the waters of the stream, I found little light, and less as I fell deeper into the earth. I looked for Anjou, but could not see him. When my thoughts told me I must take in wind again, I headed for the air and the light of the sun. With my head above the swirling waters, I saw a touch of Anjou's dark hair, moving down closer to the waters of the Lake, nearing the Rock of the Feathered Ones. My thoughts told me that I must go back into the deep and head for the Rock. Anjou must not be allowed to go that far. Others had gone there and disappeared into the earth, never to be seen again. My thoughts also told me that I too, could disappear into the earth near the Rock as others had done, but Mutee's words returned to me. "It is not his time..."

I took in wind once more. With all the power that Tarantee could give me, I threw myself forward in the waters. As soon as the darkness had covered me, my thoughts showed me Condly carrying Anjou in the darkness, holding him out for me, just before the Rock of the Feathered

78

Ones. I flew in the waters to her as fast as I could. Anjou's arms and legs drooped and his eyes closed. His body turned around and began to circle downward, just before the Rock. I knew this was the time that I must take him back to the air, the light, and the mist, before he walked too far down into the earth to return to his mother and his father. I pushed forward into the darkness and grabbed his arm, pulling it toward the light. But the earth was asking for him too, pulling him down. I saw leaves and thin branches swirling into the dark, deep waters, with the shadow of the Rock just above it. I looked up at the light and the Rock, and saw a small ledge nearby. With one hand pulling Anjou, the other grabbed for the ledge, with the light and the mist waiting for us just above. As I pulled up on the Rock, I could feel the earth giving up its grasp of Anjou as a fire burned in my arms, my legs, and my chest. I found a spot on the Rock to push upward with my feet. As I did, I threw Anjou's body into the morning air. I followed and felt the coldness of the wind breathing hard upon my head. Mutee stood right above me on the Rock, her arms stretched toward me, feathered ones swirling above her head. She caught Anjou under his arms and pulled him to the safety of the Rock's flat surface.

"Give me your hand, Caterin, and I will pull you up!" She said this in a voice that played just as much as it did when we were leaping across the rocks. Several Little Ones stood behind her. I reached out for her hand and felt the strength of her arms pull me up as I slid onto the Rock, the stream licking my legs. Anjou lay on the Rock, throwing out the part of the stream that he had taken into his body. It returned from within him to travel with its sisters in the stream down to the lake. I lay still on the Rock, enjoying its firmness, thanking it for holding us in the light, above the Other World.

"Anjou, can you speak?" Mutee asked lifting his head into her arms. The Lake flew from his mouth and he opened his eyes weakly, looking deeply into Mutee's. He did not speak.

"He will come back to us in a little while, Caterin," Mutee said as she turned to me. "It is the light that you took into the earth that he will follow back to us. Rest now, while he empties the waters of the stream from within him. I will take the Little Ones with me to the Village and bring you both blankets to hold the warmth of your blood. Rest now." She disappeared over the rocks, calling to the Little Ones to follow her. I stayed, lying on the Rock next to Anjou's shaking body.

After a short while Mutee returned to cover us with blankets. By that time, Anjou had opened his eyes, but could not keep them open, returning again and again to darkness. Mutee wrapped him in a blanket and picked him up. She carefully stepped from the Rock of the Feathered Ones to other smaller rocks in the midst of the stream. After Mutee reached the bank, she carried Anjou back to her hut. A fire welcomed us all into its warmth. Once she had

80

laid Anjou to rest, Mutee spoke to me. "Caterin, when you swam into the waters of the stream, you walked into the earth and returned to us. It is the way your child journey has begun. It will not be long now before you cross the waters of the Lake alone."

My Friend, I knew in my heart and my thoughts that Mutee spoke as the sun rose. I could feel strength as I arose from the waters of the stream that I had never felt before. I began to make words to tell my father of my plans to go alone across the Lake. I leave you now, My Friend, but I will talk again with you soon.

My Friend,
Mutee has asked me to bring you along this sun time. It has been many sun times since Anjou fell into the waters of the stream. Now he laughs and runs across the rocks as before, but with eyes that look to each new rock rather than to the sky. Mutee says that she wants me to talk with you when we have finished a short journey this sun time. She says we are climbing Tarantee to her secret place to see her flowering stone and her own wooden friend. We begin now, in the cool mist. I will talk with you when the sun stands higher.

My friend,
We have come to Mutee's secret place. Mutee does not want me to tell you of the path up Tarantee that we took to her place. It is the

place of only her. No one has been here but Mutee. She says that I may tell of what I see here though.

My Friend, when Mutee spoke of showing me her flowering stone, my thoughts saw the stones near the stream that feed the Lake of Deep Waters. When we walked into her secret place, and she showed me her flowering stone, my eyes could not catch all the light that streamed forth. Her stones beamed far brighter than the stone that Kalfiet shone for me in his hut. Mutee's stone held the light of the sun in its heart, and returned it to the mists in many colors. It was in the shape of a ring that Mutee wrapped around her neck. "Caterin," she began, "This is my flowering stone. It is growing as my heart grows in understanding the One who holds Condly and all of us."

Then, Dear Friend, Mutee did something that my eyes looked upon, but my thoughts had never seen. When she hung the flowering stone upon her neck, it grew into her, from around her neck down to her heart. It had become a part of her! Her face shone like the light of the sun on the waters of the stream and the many colors filled the walls of this place inside Tarantee.

"Caterin, this is the flowering stone that tells me of the words of Condly, growing in my heart. As the words of Condly take root in your heart and grow, so too will a flower of stone grow, and take root in you." She walked across the room and sat down at the mouth of her hut, looking out over the Village, the stream and Lake below, and far in the distance, the Great Family of Trees. "Sit with me for a moment, Caterin."

I sat next to her, and we looked together over the world I knew. The sun passed through the sky close above. We sat quietly for a long time, listening to the wordless beauty of our hearts, the ring, and our world. As I looked at Mutee and the ring, I felt the questions of my heart melt away as the white blanket does when the wind breathes warm. I had no words to say. Finally, as the sun was closing his eyes and dark time was approaching, I asked. "Can you tell me what is beyond the Great Family of Trees, Mutee?" I looked at her face as it lighted the stone walls around us, streams of light flowing from her eyes as she returned my look.

"Here in my secret place is MY wooden friend, Caterin, just as you have yours. If you wish to know what I have seen, you may listen to my friend in the next sun times to come, but only here, in this place. No others know of this place, and it must remain so. The place of my heart is known only to those who will understand it. For this dark time, I will stay here. I must return to the Little One and the Old Ones while you stay here, but I will come back to visit in those times when you send a message to my heart. You may listen to my wooden friend in the mist time when the sun has opened his eyes again." My heart leaped to know that I might understand the heart of Mutee, and I longed to listen to her stories. After we sat together watching the darkness grow, Mutee walked to her closed eye mat, and I spoke with you. Now, though, My Friend, I must close my eyes. I will talk with you again.

My Friend,
When I opened my eyes in the early light, Mutee was, without words, looking out over the village and beyond, just at the door of her secret place. Her upturned face seemed to have light within it, like tiny streams within her had grown from the stone flowers around her neck and heart. She was the most beautiful creature my eyes and thoughts have ever known. I sat next to her until the mists had returned to the Lake.

Rising, she told me I could now listen to the stories, held by her wooden friend who is like you. She walked to a rock nearby and began talking to her wooden friend, while I listened to the stories from long ago held by her wooden friend.

The stories of Mutee's child journey and beyond gave light to my thoughts, but I cannot tell them to you. Mutee says these are her stories, and that only my stories must you hold. Her stories tell of many things that the sun of this village has never seen. Many things I heard from Mutee's friend, but my thoughts could not hold them because they are so far beyond what my thoughts have known.

As the darkness gathered around Tarantee, Mutee arose from her place on a rock and sat next to me as I listened to her friend.

"What my friend tells you now, will plant the seeds of knowing in your heart. When your eyes see these things face to face, your thoughts will know them well, and your heart will be able to hold them as the sun rises. I will go down now to play with the Little Ones and hold the Old and Broken Ones. You are to stay here, and make a place in your heart for Condly." With that, Mutee slowly removed the stone flowers from her neck and placed it in a corner on one of her bundled talks. Then she wrapped me and held me in her feathered arms for a long time. Just before she left the mouth of her secret place, she turned to me.

"Long have you listened to your heart with my help. Now you will listen alone to know what your heart tells you to do, Caterin. I take my place among those with whom my life is woven. From this moment, you must walk alone for a time." She walked around the jutted rock that hid the door to her secret place, and began her climb down Tarantee.

"I will speak with you again, Mutee," I said. I watched her as long as I could see her, winding her way down Tarantee. I knew then, My Friend, that finally the child journey from my village to Condly would really begin. I stopped listening to Mutee's wooden friend long enough to look over the village of my childhood, to follow the stream

85

down Tarantee to the Lake of Deep Waters that it fed, and to the Great Family of Trees, far away. "I am ready to come to you," I said out loud to my heart and to Condly. I will talk with you again soon My Friend.

My Friend, Like Mutee's Friend,
I have spent several sun times here in Mutee's secret place, listening to her friend, my thoughts, and my heart. After I finished her stories, I longed to see Mutee, to play with the Little Ones, to help the Old and Broken Ones, and talk with my Father. But my heart told me that I must empty my thoughts of these to carry new ones on my journey. I know that I can take my Father, Mutee, and the others with me in my heart, but my thoughts must wear them as a feathers upon my arms, not as heavy rocks around my neck and my heart. More than once in these sun times and dark times, I touched the feather tied around my neck, longing to hear the words of Condly, longing to see her as the sun rises. Many dark times, I could not close my eyes because the thoughts of my heart wanted to be heard. When I have emptied my thoughts, I will speak with you again, My Friend.

My Friend Who waits for me,
It has been many sun times since Mutee walked from her secret place, leaving me alone here. The cold times are here now, and I make fire or stay inside to keep from the breath of the wind. I remember many of Mutee's words, our

times with Tomat, Kalfiet, and the Little Ones. I remember my trip into the earth through the stream, bringing Anjou back with me. I remember some of Mutee's stories, stories of her journeys. Sometimes, as I look out from her door, I remember nothing. I see the village, the stream, the trees, even Tarantee, all as tiny as the feather around my neck, held in one feathered hand, full of the light of Mutee's flowering stone, the laughter of Little Ones, and the song of birds.

It was in this morning's mist that a voice called to me, carried by the droplets from the Lake below to Mutee's secret place.

"It is time to tell your Father," the voice said to my thoughts. "It is time to walk alone to the land of Condly." I knew the voice was telling me that which rose with the sun. I knew it was the time. Now I tell you that I leave this place to talk to my Father of the journey to come. After that, I will take my place upon the raft and go to greet the Great Family of Trees and the furred and feathered Ones who live within its protection. I will talk with you again after I have spoken to my Father, My Friend who listens carefully.

My Friend,
I spoke with my Father during the last sun time and dark time. I walked to the growing place with him, even as the mists were still blanketing the earth and the sun had not yet risen and opened his eyes. "Father," I said as we

walked along the path under the trees, "It is time that I go from here, to the land beyond the Family of Trees."

"No!" he answered, in a voice that shook as bubbling water within him. "It is time you took your place next to me, here in the growing place every sun time. You have had enough time with Mutee, with the Little Ones, and the Old Ones. You have taken your light to them each sun time; it is time you brought it here." He looked at me with eyes that brimmed as the Lake banks after many times of falling waters. "You disappeared into Tarantee with Mutee many sun times ago without telling me of such travel. When she returned, Mutee told me that you would return when you had finished. Now that you return, you say that you are to leave again? And when would you return to me?" He raised his arms high, as though talking to the mist. "Are you meaning to take her too, as you did my wife, and my sons?" He turned again to me.

"No, No, No!" His voice rolled. "You must stay here and work by my side in the growing place. Your child journey can wait as mine has. Thretting cannot have you! I will not let you go!" This he said with a voice of the dark clouds. Then he sat on the ground and hid his face from me in his hands. "Go back to the house now and wait for me. Go!"

But something in my heart grew strong like the running waters jumping over the great rocks in the stream. Something told me that I must

88

stand by my Father's side this sun time, as my mother would have, and touch his heart with feathered hands. "No, Father. I stay this sun time by your side. I will not return as a Little One to the house. And I must go on my child journey. My heart is ready for the journey as the earth is ready for your hands and seeds when the wind breathes warm. The seeds have already been planted in my heart; they must see the light of my journey and not be hidden in the dark by working in the growing place each sun time. I must leave, but I will return to you after my journey is ended, and I have seen Condly face to face."

My father looked up at me, his eyes red. "You will not meet Condly on your journey! Thretting awaits you in the darkness of the Family of Trees. There you will go down into the earth, and I will see you no more! Does not your heart see this as I do? Can you not see that Mutee says words that do not rise with the sun? She was not like us after her child journey and even more after my brother, her husband, walked into the earth. She plays with the Little Ones and spends her sun times with the Old Ones or goes to some place in Tarantee for many sun times. She does not know Thretting because her thoughts refuse to see what rises with the sun. She is weak." With this, he turned screaming and hunted a tree with his hands, over and over, until blood dripped from them. He stood silent, heavy.

When he turned back to look at me, his heavy eyes made a road to mine. "My thoughts

89

had hoped that you would see her weakness, that you would see my strength, and that your thoughts and heart would turn to going to the growing place each sun time. My thoughts saw you growing to the size you are this sun time so that you could join with me there until it was time for me to go into..."

He stopped suddenly as though a voice within him had grabbed his tongue. He looked into my eyes still, but his were empty. Then, he looked at the earth below us for a long time. When he spoke again, he did so without lifting his head. "I cannot keep you. You have grown beyond the Little Ones, as you have said. Thretting would be angry if I tried to hold you from your child journey, and she would find a way to punish me." He looked up at me. "But you must know that with each step that carries you further away, you are walking closer into Thretting's arms, walking closer to the door into the earth. You must know that with each step, you can also turn around, back to the light of the sun and the warmth of our village, and my plentiful growth. Certainly, your heart can see what lies ahead in such a dark journey."

When he spoke these words, I knew that my Father did not know my heart or the strength of my thoughts. Did he know how my heart had grown when I walked into the earth through the stream to bring back Anjou? Even if he did not believe in Condly, could he not believe in Caterin?

90

"Father, you speak as the sun rises, but you also see shadows that have no life. I will go as my heart tells me. To keep me would be to walk me to the door of the earth and make me sit there as my lifetime walks away. This much you know. You too, walked on your child journey. Did you not follow the voice of your heart to the darkness of the Tree Family's shade? Did you not follow it that far before you turned around?" Just then, a small feathered One landed between us. My father looked down at it, then up at me. His eyes brimmed again. He reached for my head with feathered hands and touched his lips to my hair.

"Caterin, I can see that your heart has already flown from the nest. My heart has a hole that grows ever larger with what you say. But I cannot hold your heart from flying. My heart says only that it wants you to fly back to me after you have seen the beauty of the tree tops. To have you walk into the earth now would fill all of me with the hole in my heart. It would swallow me. I would live in the darkness of Thretting's shadow the rest of my lifetime." He took my hand, and we walked to the growing place to work side by side, my father looking heavier than I have ever seen him.

We worked side by side that sun time, without words. As the dark gathered around us on the walk to our house from the growing place, I talked with him about when I would leave. He asked me to stay until the wind breathed warm and the sun regained its strength again. "Your journey would be easier if you waited until then," he said with the voice of a mother.

"Yes, Father, these words speak to my heart. I will wait with you through the cold times and leave with the first breath of warm wind." For a moment, his face upturned, even as the rest of him grew heavier.

My Friend, I will speak with you again when we no longer go the growing place, when we rest as the wind breathes cold outside the warmth of our houses. I will speak with you again.

Dear Friend, as I walked with Mutee in this dark time, I told her what had happened between my father and me near his growing place many sun times ago, when the wind was beginning to breathe with cold.

"Your father sees Thretting waiting for you; this is what the thoughts of his heart see. If he could only see Condly, he would know..." Mutee looked up at Tarantee. "But the earth of his heart is still being prepared. Your leaving will turn over the soil and loosen the hardness within. This much I can see."

"What is it that you see, Caterin?" She asked me as she stopped before the house of my father. She spoke as a Little One, asking for something that her thoughts could not create.

92

"I see my father with an upturned face, walking with you, Mutee. I see Condly as I saw her when she held Anjou under the waters of the stream. I see myself walking through the Great Family of Trees, alone, but with my Father, with you, with the Little Ones, and the Old Ones as feathers, lifting my feet to fly with each step. That is what I see." The streams in Mutee's face filled with light.

"The flower of stone in your heart is growing, my Child. Its beauty is a wonder to see." That is what Mutee said to me, Dear Friend. I will speak with you again.

My Friend,
The wind breathed warm this sun time. I return now to speak with you for a short while in this sun time, My Friend. The cold times with my Father passed quickly. I spent most of my sun times as I had before, with Mutee, the Little Ones, and Old Ones. I spent the dark times with my Father, talking with him and building a road between our hearts. Also, Mutee came many times to visit at the house of my Father to take in some of his growth and to share some of hers with us. My heart wanted to dance when she would come there to talk with both of us. My father seemed to grow lighter as the sun times passed and we talked.

But this sun time, when I spoke of the warm breath of the wind, he drew a long breath

93

himself, losing some of the lightness he had gained. I tried to help his heart.

"Father, please remember. I go soon, as you know I must, but I will return to you. This you may hold as a flowering stone in your heart." He did not answer with words, but held me, with arms that had become feathered over the cold times. He touched his lips to the top of my head again and again.

I walked up here to visit with you, My Friend, one last time before I begin on my journey alone to the land of Condly. I wanted to talk with you, so you know that when I return, I will do as Mutee did. I will tell you everything from my journeys beyond. So, I go now my friend, without you to talk with, except in a room of my heart.

Until I return, I remain your Friend. I will talk with you again.

Grace looked up and around the cave at each of us as she finished this bundle. The Professor sat up straight, stretching his arms high as he did. "Quite interesting, very interesting, indeed. The more you read, Grace, the more I want to know." I saw that the Professor wanted to keep on reading, but I was getting very hungry, and I sensed that the rest of the group was restless as well.

"Let's stop for lunch now," I said, looking at the Professor, then at Grace.

"I would prefer that we continue, Diana." The Professor looked anxious, like he thought that stopping for lunch would somehow make the remaining bundles disappear.

"But I'm getting really hungry, Dr. Sitzer. What about you folks?" I turned and asked the rest of the group, hoping for them to agree with my stomach. No one spoke a word. It was as though they were numb. It was Grace who broke the silence.

"We should eat and take a break, Professor. We can continue after we have all had a chance to stretch, eat, and think through what we have heard so far." She said this looking directly and unflinchingly at Dr. Sitzer. Like a lost puppy, he shrugged his shoulders and nodded.

"I guess you're right. A few minutes won't matter one way or the other. OK, Everybody, let's get to it." At these words, the group awakened and stirred to life. Rising and stretching, they headed for the backpacks near the mouth of the cave. I grabbed a couple of sandwiches and a drink and headed out to sit on the ledge where Steve was eating his lunch.

"What do you think, Diana?" He asked me the question and looked away to the valley below, almost as if the question itself scared him.

95

"I don't know, Steve. It sounds like Dr. Sitzer found something extremely unusual and the more Grace reads, the more I feel that way."

"You know," he responded, "I agree with you. This journey stuff doesn't sound like the typical initiation rites for adulthood, and that stone necklace that Grace is wearing, I keep seeing it all the time in my head, whether I am looking at it or not. What else do you think she can do with it on?"

"You mean Grace?" I asked, wanting to make sure who he was talking about.

"Yeah, I mean...She sure hit the nail on the head when she talked with me yesterday...and the wind blowing each time she talks...and knowing how to read some ancient language like she was reading Huck Finn...it's incredible, beyond belief! Do you think anyone will believe us when we tell them?" With this he shook his head, then took another bite on his sandwich, something real to which he could cling.

Out from the cave walked Ryan. He wasn't wearing his usual mischievous look; in fact, he looked quite serious. "You know," he joined in, "Grace told me that when my parents divorced, and Dad moved out, I hurt so bad, and needed so much love that I just hid myself. I don't quite understand it, and I've been racking my brains trying to figure out just what she means. And that stuff about Caterin diving into that stream to save that kid from drowning; it sounds so familiar...I just can't place it."

"Ryan, I think that bump on your head yesterday broke your funny bone," I said, trying to lighten up the conversation. These guys were getting rather freaky with me. Besides, I never could deal very well with people being serious for too long. "You know, maybe this whole thing is about witches, and this ring is like a broom." They both gave me dirty looks.

"Diana, you really don't get it, do you?" Ryan was certainly not sounding like himself. "This isn't about witches and brooms, and magic, and it's not silly or stupid. This is real stuff, deep stuff. Like I said, I can't put my finger on it, but all this sounds really important, like I want to soak up each word that Grace reads. Don't make it sound like it's just fun and games, 'cause it's not." Ryan looked at me like I had just dropped one of his best term papers in the garbage.

"OK, OK. I hear you. Just lighten up a bit will you? I'm just not used to you being so serious." Steve looked like he was about to say something when Grace walked, or should I say, flowed, out to the ledge with us.

"It's beautiful out here, isn't it?" She asked, speaking to no one in particular. The two guys nodded agreement, but I had questions to ask Grace.

"Grace, doesn't that thing hurt?" I pointed to the neck ring.

"No, Diana. It looks like it would, doesn't it? In fact, it feels very comfortable, like someone wrapped one of those feather shawls around me. As for the other question on your mind, I don't mind telling you what I think." It's funny that she mentioned that I had another question because I had been wondering for quite a while just what she thought about all that had happened, from her perspective. I hadn't asked her that question out loud, but her knowing other people's thoughts was getting to be quite normal in the midst of everything else that was happening.

"OK, tell me first what my question is, and second, what your answer is." I looked at the guys, and nodded my head to remind them of what I had said about the witchcraft stuff.

"Well, the main question in your mind right now is about the power of the ring, and how I feel about it all," she said with quiet confidence. "As to an answer, I'm still not quite clear on it all. It doesn't feel like magic or witchcraft, like some people might think." I felt my face redden as she said this. The guys both gave me the dirty looks again. Grace kept talking. "It feels more natural, like this is the way things are really supposed to be, when everything is going right. It's almost like I've been looking at life through distorted, rose colored glasses before, so I've never understood who I really am, or what the world is really like, until I took off the glasses. I guess that's the best way that I can describe it. I feel as though I can see clearly now how I must live since I am wearing the ring. I also feel like I am living Caterin's life in my mind as I read it. It doesn't feel like someone else's journal or a diary; it feels like my own life. You know what I mean?" What she said sounded sincere enough, although I really didn't quite understand how and why wearing this thing around her neck could change reality. I was willing to give it a try, though, and explore it more before I made up my mind about it entirely.

"Yeah, I guess I understand a bit what you mean, but I'm still not sure about the glasses bit. Maybe after I've heard more about what Caterin does on her journey, I'll get the picture."

I didn't see Dr. Sitzer as he joined us on the ledge and spoke. "You know, I am most curious to discover more about Condly and Thretting." "It's very interesting that one person could have two names, based on how each villager perceived the person. But I guess since the person did not live among them, this kind of thing might happen quite easily." It was Steve who responded to the Professor's curiosity.

"You know Professor, it seems to me quite easy for a group of people to have different perceptions of a powerful figure such as Condly. I've had lots of coaches who were hated and loved by different members of the same team, and each group had its nick name for him."

"I'm sure that's true, even with professors." Dr. Sitzer returned. "Still I am anxious myself to find out if Caterin ever does meet either of them. Are you all feeling up to continuing now? The rest of the group is already seated and ready inside." Everyone showed their agreement with his suggestion by rising almost simultaneously and walking into the cave. The remaining members of our group were already sitting together in quiet discussion that halted as soon as Grace stepped in the cave behind me.

"Shall we begin again?" the professor asked us all. With a few murmured OK's and yes's, we all settled into somewhat comfortable positions to listen to more of Caterin's diary. Then Grace sat in her spot again, smiled broadly at the Professor, picked up another wooden slat, and addressed us all.

"This looks like the 5th bundle of writings. I believe that what we are about to read is a bit different from what you have heard before."

"Yes," interrupted the professor. "That is true. It appears that a different kind of wood and color of ink was used in this bundle. The writing also appears to be much clearer and neater. I trust that this is also Caterin's writing, but we won't be sure of that until we read some of it. Sometimes when one finds such written histories, they are composed by several people. However, since this appears to be a more personal narrative, there is a better possibility that it is all Caterin's. Well, let's take a further look, shall

100

we?" He looked at Grace as though giving his permission to continue.

"Yes, I'll continue if everyone is ready." Since everyone sat waiting and no one mentioned any reason to delay, Grace began again.

BUNDLE 5

MAKING THE NEW PATH MY FRIEND

My Friend of long waiting,

It has been many cold and hot times since I have spoken with you in this, our secret place, in Tarantee. I have held words for you within a room of my heart throughout all my journeys. When I first arrived back here in the village of my father and Mutee, I listened to what you had remembered for me, of the time before my leave-taking, alone on my child journey. Now, I want to share with you some of what I have lived, and who I have become. I have much to say, much to tell you, My Friend, from the time that I left you in the warm breath of the wind, until now. Please sit quietly while I begin where I left off, so that you may see my times as they happened, as sure as the sun rises.

The sun time that I left my little village lives in my heart and thoughts as though it happened just before this morning's mist. After I left my secret place, I stopped to tell Mutee and the Little Ones that I was leaving. She and they wished to see me begin at the bank of the Lake, so they followed me to my Father's house and on toward my leaving place. When I entered my father's house, I reached for him with my own feathered touch, reminding him of the flower of my returning that I had planted in his heart. My Father, too, wanted to see me over the waters of the Lake. So, on the sun time of my leave taking, he and many of the village walked with me to the edge of the Lake of Deep Waters. Even some of the Old and Broken Ones came to the bank to hold me with feathered hands and speak to me of the wonders I would see.

Just before I was to climb onto the raft, I stepped to Mutee, the streams in her face lighted by the sun within her. Her eyes glanced all about me, as a mother of a new Little One does in the wonder of the beauty they see.

"Caterin, you are my bird leaving the nest. Your seedling breaks the earth to venture in the sun's light. You, my friend, go now on a child journey, the journey to Woman, the journey to Mingda. When I see you again, it will be that you will have words to plant in my heart, as I have planted in yours." She touched my head and hair with feathered hands, and touched my hands with her lips and with the waters that spilled from her eyes.

"No, Mutee, that cannot be. I could never give you what you have already in your heart. But I will come back to share with you as a Little Mingda, to walk again with you to the village of the Old Ones, to play with the Little Ones in the laughing stream, and by the edge of the village."

With a tap on my cheek, her eyes glowed light into mine. For a moment, I thought I saw her ring of flowering stone, glowing on her neck, her heart, and her face. But before I could see it clearly, with feathered hands, she turned me toward my Father.

He stood looking at me, his eyes spilling water on his face. He breathed deeply in the morning mist, then spoke to me.

"Caterin, I say go with my good wishes now, but my heart waits for you to return quickly. Until then, I have set aside a room in my heart, where you will talk with me; you will walk and work beside me each sun time. Each dark time, in that room of my heart, I will put my lips to your head so that you may know that my heart lives for your heart." He stopped once again to breathe as though the air was hard to catch. "Caterin, your brothers and mother watch your every step from within the earth, and will help you on your way. Call on them when you face Thretting or the dangers that she puts before you. If you should walk into the earth before your return..." He started, but could not continue. He looked down at the dark waters and the raft before us, his head and arms hanging heavy, as though from many long sun times of work in the growing place.

I lifted his head with feathered hands, and looked into his eyes. Words traveled from my lips to him that found their way from my heart.

"Father, I know that Condly awaits me, and you too. With my leaving, the earth of your heart will be stirred so that the seed of Condly's words will take root and grow. As Condly's words grow there, Thretting's will disappear. This I know, yet I know not how I know." I walked silently into his heart on the road between our eyes, and shared the words of a daughter for her Father that can never be spoken. I touched my lips to his head and turned to the Lake of Deep Waters, to the Bank, and to the raft that awaited my feet.

The raft was the same that I had shared in my first ride on those waters, with Mutee and Tomat. I climbed on, telling the waters with the arm of a tree that I wanted to go toward the opposite side, toward the wall of trees, all the while remembering my first time upon the Lake. When I had passed beyond the shade of the brother trees by the bank, passed where we led Tomat to walk into the earth, I turned to those who watched me from the shore. I sent them light from my heart until I drifted so far that I could only see them as spots upon the bank.

As I turned back again to see the direction of my journey, I looked far in the distance at the Great Family of Trees that awaited me. As I drew closer, I saw that the Trees were much larger than I could tell from the bank of my village. Their twins in the Other World stretched far into the Lake of Deep Waters. Birds flew over me, heading in the same direction as my raft. My heart danced, and I sang a song of a Little One to the birds that are her friends.

106

Too la, too la, too la, la ahhh
The sun does dance upon your flight
Your feathers light as you frisk and flow,
You dance and laugh as your feathers blow,

Breathe Wind, breathe warm,
For feathered Friends,
To far away lands and home again.
With you some time I know I will fly.
Too la, too la, too la, la ahhh

"Onward," I told the waters, "Take me to the banks of the Great Family." But so large were the waters, that even by the time the sun had traveled far behind Tarantee, and closed his eyes, I was still far out upon the Lake. As the darkness grew, I took in some of the growth from my Father and from Mutee, watching as the lights beyond the high gathered-mists peeked out from the dark blanket. Then, the mist arose from the Lake to cover all so that I could see nothing except its whiteness all around me.

Through the darkness and the mists, many noises that I had never heard rang out. Some sounded like feathered Ones, others like screaming Little Ones. Still others were barks and growls like the hunters talked about. They all seemed to be coming from the direction of the Great Family. The waters of the Lake flowed from Tarantee toward the Great Family, so, after a while, I allowed the raft to flow as it wished as I closed my eyes to rest.

When I opened my eyes again, the blanket of mist was still all around and laying on top of me. All was still and quiet. I was very close to the shore. In the early light, I could make out the forms of the trees towering high above me. The trees here seemed much larger than the ones near my village and on Tarantee. I took in some growth, then told the raft with the arm of a tree that I wanted to head to the shore. When I reached the bank, I pulled the raft into the sand and tied it to a tree for my return trip over the Lake back to my village. Birds were already singing in the morning mist. With lightness in my heart, I headed toward the rising of the sun, as Mutee had said I should.

I walked all that sun time into the home of the Great Family of Trees. I could barely see the sun climbing as I looked up through their arms. Some of the furred Ones that I had helped my Father to prepare for taking into our bodies were walking or running alive along the floor at the feet of the trees. Since I had only seen them when the light had left their bodies, my heart felt like dancing when I could see them running about their home. My father had told me many things about his hunts in the Family, but seeing this with my own eyes was very different than living his words in my thoughts. Even the flowers grew differently from those around Tarantee. They were smaller, and their colors were darker, not like the many, bright colored flowers that we could see on Tarantee. The skin of the trees was very different too. It was thicker, and harder. Some of the Great Ones had large sections with

108

the skin fallen off. On some, it looked like many sun times had dried the old skin off. Others looked like they had parts torn off, as though some huge animal had hunted it with its claws.

It was my first dark time in the Family that I remember the best. As the sun time disappeared and the dark approached, I found a high tree's arm for my closed eye time, as my father had told me to do. I climbed up, taking my growth and all that I had with me. I found a place to serve as my mat for the dark, tied myself to the tree, and closed my eyes, but it was not for me to rest with closed eye time in that first darkness.

Each time I would close my eyes, I would hear something below moving over the leaves on the ground with sure steps. I heard the beating of wings all around me, and I felt the wind from them touch me many times. My body shook as in cold times, more when I heard a creature growl down below me. Many times, I looked down and saw yellow eyes and large teeth, glinting in the dim light, waiting for me. The tree shook as each of these furred Ones tried to knock me from my mat so far above, or as they hunted the skin of the tree.

My father's words returned to my thoughts. He had said that Thretting was waiting here to take me into the earth. Was that her face on the ground below? Was it her green eyes that stared at me from the same height in another tree not too far from my own? Would she fly or climb to get me and take me into the earth? Surely, if she would take me, she would do so in the dark; it was too easy to watch for her in the sun times. I wondered what kind of creature had taken my brother Deflic into the earth. Was it one of these that crawled below my tree?

Then I looked up, seeing the little lights above the trees. My thoughts turned to Mutee, and to Condly. I had done all I could to keep Thretting and the furred Ones from helping me walk into the earth this dark time. Why then could I not just shut my eyes and rest? Then, words that Mutee had spoken to me returned to my heart.

"When you walk a new path, you must look to its ways, not your own. See how it is different from the paths you know, and walk with light in your heart as you see such differences. Make this new path your friend."

"Surely, I thought, "If I was trying to see all that is new to me here, I could make this path my friend." As my thoughts caught her words from long ago, I began to listen and look into the darkness with eyes and ears that wanted to learn of this new path. No longer did I look down at the snarling to watch for Thretting or wonder if I would walk into the earth. With Mutee's thoughts helping my heart, I listened and looked, giving names to each of the creatures that came bidding to the feet of my rest tree. Each one had its own look and sound, not shared with any others. I even saw Little Furred Ones growling with their mothers far below on the leafy ground. I looked

110

long at the eyes that sat at the same height as me in the tree nearby. After a while, I could see, faintly in the darkness, the shadow form of a great feathered one, like some that I had often seen as they flew over the Lake of Deep Waters.

And so passed the dark. It deepened as the misty blanket threw its thickness over the trees, sifting down to the ground. As the darkness filled around me, Mutee's words grew in my heart, giving me a light within to become a friend with the darkness of my new path.

I will speak more of my travels to you, My Friend.

BUNDLE 6

THE BEAST IN MY HEART

Many sun and dark times passed as I walked through the mist of the Great Family, ever heading toward the rising of the sun. Each sun time, I walked part it as the student of Mutee, seeing a new path. But the shadow of Thretting seemed to follow me as well, ever hiding, just beyond what I could see. Each dark time, I looked down from a new resting place, high above the ground, seeing many different furred Ones walking about, waiting to see if I could offer them something to take into their bodies.

There appeared one dark time a very large furred One, with thick legs, and a huge head and body. Its teeth stood like yellow knives, gleaming in the little light that shone from above the trees. Many times it stretched up my tree on two legs, reaching for me, its mouth open wide. Several times, I watched as this creature slipped off, only to return with another smaller creature hanging from its mouth. Each time, there was much screaming and growling. Each time, I could hear the tearing of fur and the crunch of bones. Always, after the struggle, this huge creature would take in the other creature just below my tree, as if to show me what he meant to do with me.

113

After the first time that I saw this, I chose a higher place and a larger tree in which to close my eyes. This huge creature never walked where I could see him during the sun time. My thoughts told me that it closed its eyes while I walked, and followed me in the dark as the dogs in our village were able to do. Though many sun times passed, this creature showed its face at the foot of the tree of my resting each dark time.

I began to think as my father did, that this might be Thretting, taking on the form of this furred One in order to walk me into the earth. Many times my father and Mutee's words would talk with each other in my thoughts. But with each sun time, my own words grew stronger than both. I wanted to know for myself, to see for myself whether Thretting or Condly lived as the Great Queen. As it was, the great beast was the one who helped me speak my own words.

It happened one sun time, that the waters of the lake gathered in dark mists over the trees, then beat down hard on the earth. The darkness appeared as deep as that of my rest time, but the sun had just begun its journey overhead when the waters, and the dark mists gathered. The darkness above also threw great lines of light into the tree tops, booming with a deep voice. I could smell fire burning in the midst of the waters that were falling. Trying to find a place to keep from the water and the lines of light, I slipped and fell over a huge tree. When I did, I could not move one of my legs. It was asleep, so I lay on the ground waiting for it to wake again. In my

114

thoughts I saw my brother Deflic, hunting among these same trees, being hunted himself by some creature. Then Deflic's face became mine, and I knew that I was close to the door into the earth.

The waters kept falling hard, the wind was breathing harder and colder, and little lakes formed near my body. I crawled under the fallen tree as much as I could. My body started shaking.

A line of light was thrown nearby, and in the flash, I saw the huge furred creature that had been following me so many sun and dark times. He was standing in the falling waters a short way from me, looking at me with eyes that I did not like. He started to walk slowly toward me, lowering his body close to the earth, his eyes making roads to mine. I pulled my sleeping leg further under the fallen tree. I looked again and saw Deflic, standing in the path between me and the beast. Even so, I could see through him to the snarling mouth and sharp teeth that wanted me. Still, my eyes searched its eyes.

I thought of Mutee's words, "Make friends with what you do not know. Find help to see all as part of the One by knowing it will be there." I remembered seeing Condly in the waters of the stream when I returned Anjou from under the earth. Now Deflic slid into the earth, and Condly slipped silently into place, walking beside this beast. Or was this Thretting? Maybe it was Thretting I had seen under the waters, wanting to carry Anjou off, and now, at last, she was coming with the beast to take me into the earth. This my thoughts told me, but my heart said no. I searched deeper into the eyes of the creature, wanting to make a road to its heart.

I remembered what I did under the earth, in the waters of the stream. I had looked into the earth and walked straight to its door, as though I had joined hearts with Condly as I searched her eyes. Now, I was at the door into the earth again, facing the eyes of the beast. It stopped walking toward me for a few breaths, staring back at me. It stopped growling.

At that moment, a line of light struck behind the creature, and a terrible crash sounded all around. As it did, I saw the beast leap toward me, racing away from an enormous tree that was falling from the flash. I could hear the tree falling toward me, smashing many arms of other trees and the bodies of small trees as it fell. In another flash of light, I saw its arms spread out, strike the ground, and trap the creature, just an arm's length from my face. The body of the fallen tree landed on the tree under which I had crawled. I heard the beast yelp in pain as one of the little dogs of our village might. He reached out with his great claws, fear flying from his eyes. One of his claws caught my sleeping leg. As he drew his claws back to try to pull himself out from the tree that held him, the skin of my leg opened, and blood poured onto the ground. I grabbed and held my leg, trying to stop my blood from leaving me. A fire started inside where the skin had torn. It kept burning, even though the

116

waters kept falling on it. At the same time, the tree held onto the creature tightly, and he stopped struggling to free himself. He whimpered softly, closed his eyes, then lay silent.

After a long time, the waters stopped falling, but darkness crowded around me. I closed my eyes to rest. If there were noises in this dark, I heard none of them. I could only feel my heart beating in the leg that had been opened, and my hand told me that the blood had stopped leaving me. I closed my eyes again and thought no more.

When next I opened my eyes, I saw the thick blanket of morning mist and the sun trying to peek through. I could see little else because leaved tree arms and the body of the fallen trees covered me. I took in some of the nuts and other gifts of the Family that I had gathered and kept in a pouch close to my body. I could see the beast just beyond my leg, but he did not move.

After I had taken in this growth, I tried moving my leg, but still it rested, not wanting to wake up. The fire in it burned less than it had, but I covered the open part with watered leaves to cool the fire more.

Mutee spoke to my thoughts, telling me to continue on my journey to Condly. To go on, I knew that my leg must wake up, and the fire inside must go out. I thought that dragging my leg to a stream might help, but I needed to

117

uncover enough of the arms of both fallen trees so I could pull myself out. As the sun traveled its long path over the tree tops, I broke off the arms that covered me, one by one, until I could see all around me.

Just before sun closed his eyes again, I had removed enough of the tree's arms to climb out. I could see the creature clearly. His body still lay under several of the strong, leafy arms of the new fallen tree. He did not move. I watched him for a long time while I was waiting for my leg to wake up. Still, he did not move. I could not tell whether he had light in him, or if he had gone into the earth.

Darkness came again, and I stayed near the body of the beast, feeling very heavy from removing all the arms of the trees around me. It was in the midst of the darkness that I awoke from hearing a sound like a Little One weeping softly. I found that my leg had awakened a bit, but still the fire burned within. I looked up and around to find from where the weeping came, but I could not. The darkness picked up the voice and flung it around the trees, so that I heard it from several places. My eyes wanted to return to rest, and so they did, shortly after hearing the cry.

In the morning mist, I felt my leg burning still. The crying I had heard in the dark continued but more softly. Looking around, I saw that it was the beast who cried. His eyes had opened a small bit, and his huge tongue hung

118

out. I could move a little, but as I did, the fire burned stronger in my leg. We lay there for a long time, the beast and I, through the morning mist and as the sun traveled across the treetops, looking into each other's eyes. He was very heavy, as though he was at the door of the earth, ready to return through it. When I peered only into his eyes, they seemed like a Little One's whose mother had left him. I wondered again whether the person that I saw next to the beast when he approached me in the falling waters was that of Condly, or of Thretting. Or was it my own brother, Deflic reaching to me from inside the earth?

Then my thoughts saw the creature standing again in the darkness of the falling waters. I saw a road grow between the creature's heart and mine; I knew that our hearts had spoken on this road, if only for a moment. He had watched me so many dark times as I rested in the tree. His claws had torn my leg. But in the moment that our hearts had spoken, his heart told me who he was, a creature that must hunt to live. When I looked into his eyes as he lay crying, his heart showed me that he had reached out with its claws in order to be free, free to live. I could leave him to walk into the earth alone, or I could mend him, like Mutee and I used to do with the Broken Ones. What would Mutee do? What would Condly speak to my heart? What did my heart want?

As I lay there, I listened to the voice of the Family of Trees, and finding also a voice in my heart, I heard the words that told me what to do. The light in the beast could be kept from walking into the earth if I would share my light with him. My heart told me that life was important, that I was here to journey with the creature for a short while, bringing him back from the door into the earth. Once I knew the direction of my path, I felt strength return to my body.

I struggled to crawl over to him, the fire in my leg burning brightly now. I carried water and gifts from of the earth with me. I cupped my hand below his great mouth, holding water to it; he touched his tongue to it. I did this several times until he moved his rough tongue to lap up the water. Then his eyes closed again for a long time. I took in some gifts and drank some. Then, my body, like his, closed to the sun for a while.

We lay like this, the beast and I, for several sun and dark times. We drank water and took in growth together. No other beasts came near. I thought it was because they knew the smell of the beast, and did not want to come near him to be hunted. They did not know that he could not hunt, or move. Each sun time, the fire in my leg burned less. Each sun time, my leg awoke a little more. Each sun time, the beast took in more earth gifts and drank more water, but he did not move any part but his head.

As much as I was able, I tried to break away the arms of the tree that held the beast down, but it was slow work, making my body heavy
120

after just a short time. Remembering what my father used to break tree arms, I knew I would need a cutter like he had to free the beast. I found a stone that would cut and wrapped it with vine to a stick. It took many sun times and much of my strength, but finally, I cleared the beast's body of the tree's powerful arms. Still, he could move just a little, raising his great head, and dropping it shortly after, closing his eyes as he did.

With the passing of many sun times and the work I had to do to free the beast, I could feel my strength and saw his returning. I thought many times of Mutee, of my father, and of my brother Deflic. On the road between our hearts, the beast told me the story of my brother. It was not Thretting who walked him into the earth, but a creature, like himself, who hungered to take in that which walked and ran. Deflic's voice seemed to speak to me from within the beast.

"It was my time to return to the earth, Caterin. Remember how I touched my lips to your head before I left the village the last time? It was such a touch for long farewells, for even then I knew, deep in my heart, that I would not return again to play with you in the sun. I am with the One who gives light to you, to this beast, to all." With that his voice stopped. Peering again into the eyes of this great beast, I saw Deflic's eyes, and the hole in my heart softened, growing a bit smaller. I stroked the head of the beast, his great body, and his legs, practicing the touch of feathered hands that Mutee had taught

121

me in a time that was beginning to seem many
life times away. With gifts from the earth and
water, as well as the touch that I offered, the
beast began to move little bits each sun time.

My leg grew strong enough that I was able
to again gather gifts from the trees and the earth
around us. I found a stream running nearby and
brought back its coolness for the beast in the
heat of the sun time. The sun time finally arrived
when the great beast himself was able to raise
his body and slowly follow me to the stream.
When he arrived there, he dropped his head at
the edge of its laughing water, and licked at it,
while the rest of his body lay as in rest again.
We stayed there several sun and dark times while
he lay at the stream, lapping at the water, eating
the gifts of the trees that I brought to him, and
resting, moving little.

Each sun time, I wandered a little farther
from where the beast lay resting. It was when I
headed toward the rising sun again that I found
how my resting leg and the beast might have
saved me from walking into the earth. As I
searched the ground for gifts of the earth to take
in, I noticed that the sound of my steps began to
come back to me. I stopped suddenly, and
stepped back when I saw why. Just before me,
hidden by the leaves of bushes was a great cliff,
like the one of Tarantee that I climbed to Mutee's
and my own secret place. Had I walked this way
in the darkness during the time that the waters
fell and the light broke from the sky, I surely

would have stumbled over the edge and into the earth.

I looked between the leaves of the bushes to the valley below. There a deep stream ran through its midst, with a wide area of grass near its banks. The green of this valley was as bright as I had ever seen, far more than the color in our village and in our growing places. I tried to find a way over the edge to climb down, but I could not see one from where I stood. I knew that I needed to find a way down, to cross this valley, and to climb the mountain on the other side of the great running water below.

I returned to the beast at the stream and fed him some of the gifts that I had found. He lifted his head weakly, and looked into my eyes. I told him that I was soon to continue my journey alone. His actions told me that my thoughts were as the sun rising, for he lifted his great body and walked a little into the bubbling stream, hunting a fish with those great jaws. He returned to the bank to take it into his body, lying with the fish's body, limp between his forelegs. My heart knew then that it would be soon that he would run again, hunt again, as he was meant to do. I felt the feather that hung from my neck move with the breath of the wind.

"The feathered Ones must fly, the tooth and claw must hunt," spoke a voice within my thoughts. As much as I wanted to walk beside the beast in his strength, to stand protected among the trees by his power, I now knew this was not to be. I must leave before he returns to his strength, so that he can live as he was created to be. It was in that moment that my thoughts found a way to live with such beasts. No longer in my thoughts did I see Thretting in the face of the beast that took my brother into the earth. Instead, I saw the face of my beast, the one who wanted to live as he was created, hunting not just to take others into the earth for Thretting, but so that he may live.

So, I walked away, leaving the beast as he took the fish into his body at the bank of the stream. I could feel his softened eyes following me as I walked through the cool, laughing waters and into the cover of the trees on the other side of the stream. As I headed in the direction of the cliff, searching along the edge for a path downward, my thoughts knew, My Friend, that the hole in my heart had grown smaller, lined on the edges by this great furred beast.

I will speak more of my travels to you, My Friend.

BUNDLE 7

I CLIMB FROM THE HOLE

My Friend Who Traveled with my Heart,
It took many sun times of searching, and many dark times resting near the edge until I found a path to lead to the bottom of the wooded cliff. I still took my dark, closed eye time in the trees, but when I heard the voice of those like my beast, my heart leapt with song instead of seeing Thretting waiting at the door into the earth. I rested deep and strong, and walked long during my sun times then.

When I finally arrived at the bottom of the cliff, I found everything here to be different than I had seen before. I found that the deep stream was much greater than the ones I had known before. Rather than the brown earth, grasses stood on its banks, soft and green. These gave way easily to my feet, causing part of my legs to sink into the grass. Many, many white feathered Ones fed in these grasses, flying to other grass areas at my approach. Other tiny winged creatures with no feathers flew there also. These I had never seen before. Some of these featherless Ones hunted my skin as they swarmed around me in great numbers. My thoughts told me that I had walked into their home, and that I must take as little time here as possible.

125

Even the air was different here. The mist still blanketed the dark. But the wind breathed earlier in the sun time with more strength than near Tarantee. This made the mist go away while the sun was just beginning its journey above. The sun showed much greater strength here than in my village.

The stream before me had grown larger from what it was while I stood on the cliff looking down. The voice of this one was quiet, its power showed mighty as its waters sped quickly on. I looked deeply into it, drank from its waters, and rested in the soft grass banks after my journey down the cliff. I knew that I could not walk across this as I had done in the stream where I had just left the beast, nor was it like the stream from which I had pulled Anjou under the shadow of Tarantee. I knew that I would need to build a raft like the one that carried me across the Lake of Deep Waters. It took many sun times to finish, but at last, I had a raft that looked like the one that helped me begin my journey alone.

When I had pushed my raft into the running waters, away from the grassy bank, I climbed on and floated with the deep stream, telling it as I did that I wanted to go toward the rising of the sun. The running waters carried me far along. I saw many different trees and creatures on the way. Never had I seen such creatures as those who drank from the waters of this stream. Still, the great mountain stood on the other side, waiting, calling me to climb over its white head,

126

to see the lands that lay beyond its heights.
Finally, with much urging, my raft found its way
to the sandy bank on the other side of the
stream.

I rested as soon as I landed on the far side,
even though the sun was high and dark time far
away. It was hard to find a soft place to rest as I
had found on the other side. This side was filled
with rock from the mountain that stood above.
When I opened my eyes again, the darkness, and
the sounds of the creatures that walked in its
protection, surrounded me. My thoughts told me
to walk slowly in the darkness because of the
great strength of the sun's power here. This I
did, climbing the mountain, looking for paths to
take toward the white head that shone above.

Here there were few trees, and these were
bent and worn like the Old and Broken Ones
whom I had helped many sun times with Mutee.
These trees stood on the side of the mountain,
often alone in the middle of many huge rocks,
some the size of my father's house. Finally, I
found a small, laughing stream to follow up the
mountain. Here, I found more trees, smaller
ones with large leaves. I drank often from the
stream's cool waters. I knew that this stream
would lead me to the mountain's head.

Still, during the sun times, I tried to find a
tree who would offer its shade to protect me
while I closed my eyes. In the dark, I climbed,
using my eyes, my hands, and my feet to see the
way to go. As each dark time passed, and as I

neared the white head of the mountain, it was harder for my mouth to catch enough wind. I stopped many times just to breathe, to look at the valley below from where I had come, and to listen to the beauty of the sounds in the dark.

It was after just a few suns from my crossing the great stream, that my body told me that it was broken. There were many bumps on my skin, which had turned bright red; a fire started there and grew inward. My body felt heavy and wanted to rest all the time, even in the coolness of the dark. I wanted to take nothing into my body. I stopped climbing. Then, one dark time, my thoughts turned to my mother and my brother Dadock as I felt a fire burning deep within me. I crawled to make a resting spot in the laughing stream, allowing the laughing waters to leap over my body. I closed my eyes for a long time.

When I opened my eyes again, the fire had filled all of me. I felt my arms, my head, my legs; they were all on fire. My body did not want to move, except to drink from the waters of the stream. Even this took a long time, and I closed my eyes and rested after the water had filled me. Many times, when I closed my eyes, I could see my Mother, lying on a mat, the same fire burning inside her. I could see Dadock, lying in the darkness of our house, waiting to go into the earth.

I saw the door to the earth open, and watched my mother and brother walk through it

128

toward me. I saw them as clearly as the sun rises. Dadock held my mother's hand as they walked together out of the shining waters. I did not know that one could walk out of the earth like this. Was the fire in my body walking me through the door and into the earth to meet them, or had Dadock and mother actually walked out of the earth?

"Hello, my Little One," spoke my mother with a voice that seemed to rise from the laughter of the stream. Dadock reached out to me with one hand, the other holding my mother's. Both of them had upturned faces, with light streaming from their bodies. "There is nothing to fear, my Caterin. We live in the flowering light of the One. I can see the light of the One growing in your heart, Caterin; it is most beautiful."

"Caterin," Dadock spoke, his voice riding the breath of the wind, "We know that you are on your way to Condly. You have come to this place to visit us, but you must finish your journey. I have much that I want to say to you, dear Sister. Open your heart."

As he spoke, a stream of questions flowed from my heart to my thoughts. Why is my mother not afraid? How is it that their faces are upturned and bodies so bright? Is that what happens when one goes into the earth? Can they really see and walk around as they did before they went into the earth? Did they finish their child journeys there? Many times, Mutee had mentioned the One who lived in all, but was it the same One that Dadock mentioned? Did Condly too, live with the One? More and more questions arose in my thoughts, but Dadock spoke before I could ask any of them.

"Caterin, take my hand for a moment." I reached out and touched Dadock. His hand felt as soft as the mist and as feather-warm as the light from the early sun. I felt a light as bright as the sun and cool as the wind enter my body through my fingers. The light breathed through me as with ever widening circles, and I felt my thoughts flow away with the laughter of the stream. Dadock's eyes made a road to mine, and I opened my heart for wordless thoughts to travel between us. We spoke to each other like this for a long time, answering the questions of our hearts, and I felt the hole in my heart shrink and disappear.

"Dadock, I want to stay with you and with Mother. I don't want to finish my child journey. I don't need to see Condly. I don't want to walk on the earth for more cold and hot times. I want to stay right here, and share this light with Mother and with you."

Dadock spoke with the bubbling laughter of the waters. "Caterin, you will join us some day; it is not your time now. Until it is time, open your heart so that others may find their light by seeing yours." His hand slipped from mine, and with upturned faces, both he and my Mother sank back into the waters of the bubbling stream.

130

When I opened my eyes again, the darkness had arrived and the coolness of the wind's breath soothed me. I could feel the fire inside, but my heart told me that it had lost some of its power. The waters of the stream still rolled over me as I lay in its bed, my head resting on the warm bank. Then my thoughts turned again to Dadock, to my mother. Had I really seen them? Had I really touched my brother? I looked at my hand, then rested it close to my heart, closing my eyes into darkness once more.

I awoke to the sounds of feathered Ones singing nearby. There were several very small white and black ones, chasing each other as they swung from one tree to another in unseen loops, riding the breath of the wind as they flew. I did not know their song, but it brought one to my thoughts. It was the song that Mutee sang to Tomat as we carried him on the raft, the song of a new mother. I saw Mutee's face in my thoughts; I saw her singing to Tomat; I saw her singing to me. I pulled my body from the stream and lay on the bank in the sun's light that was able to slip beneath the shade of the trees. I listened to the laughing of the stream, the sound of the wind breathing through the tree tops. I watched the trees waving their woody arms to comfort me. I felt as though I was in the arms of my mother, being held safe, with the feeling that Mutee called joy, a feeling that was like the sun's light, a laugh, and the breath of the wind, deep within my thoughts. I knew the fire inside was slowly disappearing. I knew that I had lived through what had taken my mother and brother into the earth.

In the sun times and dark times that followed, I slowly took in bits of the gifts that lay around me, offered by the trees. I drank slowly from the laughing stream that had put out the fire. I thanked the stream, the feathered Ones, the trees, the sun, and the darkness. I thanked them all for holding me in feathered arms, for holding me as I struggled at the door into the earth.

Then, my heart remembered something Mutee had said about the One who held all. As from a story of long ago, I remembered the words of my mother when I saw her arise from the stream. She also mentioned the One. Was there really someone who was more powerful than Condly? Why did Mutee not tell me more about this person? Why would my mother speak of this person from under the earth? As these questions arose in my thoughts, my strength and desire to see Condly grew. I wanted to ask her these questions. I wanted to know if these thoughts rose with the sun. I will tell you more of my travels later, my Friend.

BUNDLE 8

I STAND ON THE MOUNTAINTOP

I stayed by the stream under the comfort of the trees for many sun times until my full strength returned. The wind was beginning to breathe hard and cold once again. I did not know how the waters of the lake would fall, and how cold it would become in this place. Still, I was anxious to go on with my journey now, rather than wait until the fresh breath of warm winds should come again.

Climbing the mountain by following the stream became easier and easier as the stream grew smaller. Since the sun had grown cooler, I walked in the light now instead of the dark. It was just a few sun times after I started again that I found the mouth of the mountain where the stream flowed out. I rested there and drank this water coming directly from the mountain, but, I did not stay long. The head of the mountain stood larger and closer, calling me to its height. There lived fewer and fewer trees in this place, near the head, so I walked fully in the light of each sun time and closed my eyes under the lights beyond the darkness.

Covering the rocks at the head of the mountain was a white blanket like that which fell on our village in the cold times. Drops of water fell to the earth as I held some of it in my hand. This white water held the cold breath of the wind in it. It was much harder to walk on than the rocks. I slipped and fell many times as I tried to keep my feet where I planted them, but soon I learned how to walk without falling.

It took just a few sun times for me to reach the head of the mountain after arriving at the place covered by the white blanket. The wind breathed often here, and cold too, but I was warmed by my thoughts of meeting Condly, by thoughts of what lay beyond the head of the mountain, and by the thought of Mutee's feathered hands.

When I arrived at the very top of the mountain's head, I looked all around me. It was a most beautiful sight! Looking back, I could see the Great Family of Trees beyond the cliff that I had climbed. Toward the rising of the sun and far away, I could see a great lake that washed to the end of the earth. Touching this great water were more mountains that stretched in another direction. Before the great lake, was a great flat area, with trees growing in small clumps, and golden grass covering most of the earth there.

On the flat area roamed great numbers of animals that I had never seen before. I could not see them well from the head of the mountain, but I could tell that there were great numbers of them, moving about in the grasses. Far off, in the midst of the grasses stood a group of trees, huddled together. Just beyond it lay what looked like a growing place, just like that of our villagers.

I stayed on the head of the mountain, looking all around me far into the dark time. At last, I grew tired and lay down to close my eyes. When the sun arose again, I could barely see it because a thick mist blanket had surrounded the head of the mountain. As much as I liked watching the animals, the grasses, and the great lake before me from this height, my heart directed me to climb down and head across the flat lands.

Had I found the home of Condly at last? I did not know what I would find when I came to the land of Condly. I had seen her house in my thoughts, a very large house, larger than any in our village. Her village would be a very large one, with many houses and people. But was it near a mountain? Near a clump of trees? In a hidden valley? Or here on this grassy flat? As I climbed down the mountain, my heart longed to find her soon.

I walked quickly down the mountainside, following a path that I was able to see from the mountain's head. It took only a few sun times and dark times to reach the foot of the mountain. My heart leapt so much inside that I rested but a little, wanting to move onward. At last I reached the flat grass land.

As I walked toward the rising of the sun, I looked closely at the animals that I had seen from on the head of the mountain. Some were

135

striped, some wore horns like the goats of
Tarantee, but they stood much larger. A small
number were so tall that they were eating leaves
from the tops of the few trees. Feathered Ones
in great numbers flew from spot to spot in the
grasses. Nowhere did I see any like my beast in
the Family of Trees. I did not know whether the
creatures that I saw hunted, so I stayed away
from them, but not so far that I could not see
them as they walked about. There were a few
scattered rocks, large enough for me to climb and
see the groups clearly. With just a few trees, I
knew that I would need to move on in order to
find gifts of the earth to take in. I did not see
any sign of villages, or houses there among the
beasts.

As the sun times and dark times grew colder
and the sun spent less time traveling above, I
kept walking. I had run out of gifts to take in for
several sun times and still, as I walked, I saw the
same grassy flat area and the same kind of
animals all around me.

It was shortly after the sun had risen again
that I found a small lake with trees, and animals
surrounding it. I still did not know whether any
of these animals would hunt to take in growth for
their bodies, but I was hungry enough to try to
find something for myself in the trees, and to
drink the water there. I slowly walked toward
the bank of the lake, staying as low as I could in
the tall grasses so that I would not be seen. A
huge gray One, with white horns that hung down
from his mouth, and with a thick tail in the front

136

and a thin one in the back, stood in the water ahead, waving his enormous ears, and swaying from side to side in the water covering his tree-like legs. I walked around to one side of the lake, sensing that he would want some space between us. I drank from the cool waters and looked on the ground below the trees along the bank for some gifts of the earth. Several that I tried, my mouth did not like, and I threw them out. But I found one that my mouth liked so I took in as many of these as I could. All the while, this huge creature was watching me, still swaying and spraying himself with the front tail.

Finally, I looked at his eyes, and tried to make a road to him like I had done with the great beast. When I did this, he stopped swaying, and met my eyes. It was but a moment, but my thoughts told me that this creature could sense my thoughts, accepting the kindness that I offered him, offering his own in return. In that brief time, he told me that no one here would harm me, that I could pass in their midst like a creature-child. His thoughts told mine that my kindness to the beast had been told as a story among other creatures, spread by the feathered Ones that had watched at the stream so far away. The feathered Ones had told that I was approaching, to make way for one so kind. I thanked him, bowing my head as I did. He bowed his head in return.

I told this kind creature that I was heading for the land of Condly and asked if he knew if I was close. His thoughts told me that there were

137

others like me toward the rising of the sun. Some walk through here as they travel to far places. Others who live on the flat lands come to this lake to hunt creatures.

I spent several sun and dark times there with these new creatures, accepting their kindness. But, as much as I liked walking among them on the banks, under the trees, and in the water, my heart kept telling me to go to the land of Condly. So I packed up many of the gifts that I found under the trees there, along with waters from the lake, and headed again toward the rising of the sun.

It was during this part of my journey, my Friend, that I found that I had been talking to someone in my heart. This someone, I could not see, yet my heart knew the presence of one who walked along with me, who carried my heart when I was weak, who danced with me in the grass and along the bank of the lake of creatures. This person spoke with words that my heart knew, but my thoughts could not hear. I cannot remember when the person had entered my heart with such words. I cannot remember when I knew for the first time that this person was with me. All my thoughts told me was that not only my face, but my heart, and my body felt upturned in the presence of this person. It was the kindness of Mutee, the protection of my father, the power of the beast, the coolness of the wind's breath, and the joy of the feathered Ones, all held within one. Who was this?

I walked for many sun and dark times now, ever more wanting to see Condly face to face. At last, I arrived at a small hut in the midst of the grass lands. There, an old man greeted me with great kindness.

"Hello, Fair One. I can tell you have come a great distance across the plains. Are you on your way to Condly?" At last I had met someone who could help lead me to the great queen.

"Yes," I said, my heart dancing to hear someone else mention her name.

"You are not far, dear Child, and yet you are not near." His eyes spoke with a kindness, yet his words my thoughts could not catch. "There is her land, at the banks of the lake that has no end. Stay here and rest a few sun times before you go." His eyes spoke from a heart that felt like Mutee's. I could only say yes to his offer.

"I will stay, Dear One. But can you speak again of where I can find Condly?"

"I will tell you after you have taken in some gifts of the earth." These words were as the sun rising, for after we had taken in gifts together in his hut, we walked out into the darkness, and he began. "Condly's land is just beyond the land of the Hunters. She is a great queen, but the Hunters have long spoken of her as a child and seen her as a Broken One, even though her Visitors tell of her great kindness and power. They see, but they do not see. Their eyes are blind to her. The Hunters have the power of creatures of the earth; she has power of the sun, the wind, and the waters." His eyes lit up the darkness around him as he continued. "Condly's Visitors say her heart still rests in the midst of their words and their hunting."

"Must I pass through the land of the Hunters to go to Condly?"

"There is no land that is not the land of the Hunters, as they see it," replied the Old One. "You have already walked many sun times in the land that they hunt. There is no land that they do not hunt at some time."

"Why is this?" I asked him, Dear Friend.

"It is because no land can fill the holes in their hearts that they create as they hunt for land to fill up the holes in their hearts. So, they must spend all their sun times hunting while they spend their dark times looking into the holes of their hearts."

My heart knew what the Old Man spoke. I saw in my thoughts, a great number of people, walking in great circles, looking for things to throw into the dark holes in their hearts, faces downturned. In thinking this, my thoughts saw that the hole in my heart was gone completely! I remembered that it had closed at the stream with my brother's touch, but had it returned afterward? No, I did not see it return to my heart after that. The hole in my heart was filled!

140

"I can see that you are complete," continued the Old One. "You hold the secret that the Hunters cannot see because of their blind eyes." How did this one know what my heart felt? "Come, I will show you what your heart knows, but your thoughts must see." He led me back to his lone hut standing in the midst of the grasses of the great numbers of creatures.

He reached below his mat, pulling out a neck ring like the one Mutee had worn. He placed it on his shoulders. I watched as the sparkling light replaced the darkness of his hut, and the glowing flowers of stone spread from the ring, into his body, filling his face, his shoulders, and his heart with light.

"Yes, I too am a Mingda, as your friend Mutee. The Visitors have brought me word of you and of her for many cold and hot times from across the lands that you walked."

I looked at the ring of light. "But why must you and Mutee keep such beauty hidden? Why can you not show the Hunters so that their hearts be filled with the light?" I had not thought of Mutee's words for many sun times, but the Old One spoke them as his own.

"The earth of their hearts is not yet ready. There will be a time when the seed the One has planted in the darkness will grow when the earth of their hearts has softened. Then, they too, will have hearts filled with flowering stone, rather than dark holes. We all carry the seed, but few tend the earth of their hearts to grow it well. Now they would see magic in the flowering stone instead of the joy in our hearts. Keep in your thoughts, my Hearted One, that this ring is magic that is not magic." With that, he removed the neck ring, and placed it back under his mat. When he returned to speak with me again, his body was still glowing with the light. "The neck ring grows as the heart is filled with light. It is a way of looking into our hearts." I touched the feather hanging from my own neck, and saw Mutee in my thoughts, speaking to me of feathered hands, and the light of our hearts.

"My heart knows." I said this to the Old One before my thoughts could speak. Even as I knew what he spoke, I also knew that I must pass through the land of the Hunters to go to Condly, but I did not know, My Friend, that my longest walk lay ahead. I did not know before I left the Old One, that I would learn to grow light in darkness.

I will speak more of my travels to you, My Friend.

BUNDLE 9

HUNTED HEARTS

My Friend Who Listens Closely to my Words,
    As I left the door of his hut in the cold, early sun, the Old One put his arms around me, holding me as my father had when I was a Little One. Then he stood back, his eyes making a road for thoughtless words between our hearts. Finally he spoke.

"Condly waits for you. Keep in your thoughts that as the light spreads under your feet, it lights the way for others as well. Walk now, as always, with the One." Now he, too, had spoken of the One. I wanted him to tell me more.

"Who is this One you and Mutee speak of? Does Condly know of the One? Where does the One live?"

"You know the One yourself, Child. I cannot tell you what your heart already knows. Walk now, and ask your heart these questions." With that, he bowed his head deeply, and with upturned face, stood silently as I left him.

I headed toward the great lake with no end as the Old One had told me. As I walked, the land changed. The creatures disappeared, and I saw but a few that were hiding behind rock or

143

tree. I saw great areas like the growing place of my village, only much larger. I saw trees in great numbers, hunted to lie on the ground. It was the cold time now, and I knew that no one would walk to the growing places that I passed, but my thoughts saw great numbers of people here when the wind breathed warm again.

It was at the bank of a stream that I first saw the group of Hunters. As I walked down to the waters to drink, they came out from behind trees. Men and women ran to surround me. They hunted me, blood running from my skin where they did. Then they grabbed me and held me tightly. I knew they were the Hunters by the looks in their eyes, even though they carried no tools to hunt creatures. They spoke to me in a language that my thoughts could not hear, but my heart knew what they said. They dragged me back to their village. The two women who I saw first were speaking in loud voices, hunting each other, blood running from several spots of their skin. I stood by, not knowing why these two treated each other as hunters treat creatures to take in for growth. Finally, one of them fell to the ground, and the other grabbed my arm and pulled me to a hut. There, she took vine, wrapping my hands and feet as I did with the arms of trees when I made my raft. I could not move so I lay still on the floor of the hut. As I closed my eyes in the dark time, I could hear more hunting outside the hut.

I wish not to tell you, My Friend who does not hunt, all that happened to me in my stay with

144

the Hunters. I was kept all that cold time, wrapped in vines, fed by the woman Hunter who grabbed me at the first. She made me work too, as she showed me. She hunted me often until my blood ran, but my heart told me as the old man had said, that she did this to fill the hole in her heart. I could see that it never filled her even as she hunted me, and I held to the flower of light growing in my heart as she did this to me. Although she made holes in my body, the hole in my heart never returned and waters never overflowed the banks of my eyes.

When the wind breathed warm again, I was led to the growing place to work as my father had, but longer, before the sun arose in the mist and beyond the time that he would go to his bed and close his eyes. This I did for two cold and hot times, staying in the house of the woman when I was not working.

As I worked, I learned the words of the Hunters. I spoke often with the woman who kept me, whose name was Thar. I told her of my child journey, of Mutee, of the Old and Broken Ones, and of the Little Ones. Most of my sun times, though, I worked by her side, listening to the words and songs that grew from the hole in her heart. They were songs that I knew could not fill the hole in her heart. My thoughts traveled often to Mutee, to my father, and to the old man who had told me to let the light of my feet light the way for others. Even as I lived in the darkness of the hearts around me, I kept my thoughts on the seeds that wanted to grow within each of the Hunters.

As I lived with Thar, her Little Ones, and her husband, I shared the way of feathered hands and voice that Mutee had shown me. I held the Little Ones with my feathered hands and sang to them the songs of the mothers of my village and the songs of light that Mutee sang to me. I laughed with the Little Hunters and danced with them along the bank of the stream.

It was in one of the cold times that Thar's Little One named Larsee walked into the earth, burning from a fire within. After the light had gone from Larsee, I held Thar with feathered arms for many sun and dark times to keep the hole in her heart from growing ever larger, ever darker. I talked to her of Tomat, of singing the song of a new mother to him as we walked him to the door into the earth. I spoke of my mother and my brothers, and what they had spoken to me at the stream while I burned from the fire within. I held Thar like Mutee had held Tomat at the bank of the Lake of Deep Waters, like a new Little One. She shook and shook, the banks of her eyes overflowing while the edges of the hole in her heart were pushed and pulled by the darkness trying to swallow her completely.

At last her eyes stopped flowing like a lake over its banks, and her shaking came only once in a while. She closed her eyes to rest, and I sang to her, hoping that the seed in her heart would begin to grow and fill the hole in her heart.

146

As the sun rose the next morning, my heart told me that the seed of her heart had begun to grow. This showed itself to be as the sun rises. No longer did Thar hunt me, or her Little Ones. The other Hunter women of the village saw this. They asked her how she could sing and laugh with me as we walked to the growing place and worked side by side. As the sun times and dark times passed, more of the Hunter women asked me to come to the side of their Little Ones as they burned from a fire within, or as their father or mother, and Old One prepared, shaking, to walk into the earth.

So, it came that as the wind began to breathe cold again, I told Thar once again of wanting to see Condly. This time, her heart was able to hear my words. Her heart had grown to hear the heart thoughts of others; she knew I must go.

In the time of my leaving, a large group in the village gathered to see me walk toward the rising of the sun. Before I left, I wrapped my arms around each of the Little Ones I had grown to know. I did the same with some of the Grown Hunters as well, telling them as I did, that part of my heart would stay there with them. This leaving was like my first leaving long ago at the bank of the Lake of Deep Waters. This was my second family, my second village, the second home to leave on my journey to Condly. Just as I had done when I left the village under the shadow of Tarantee, I left part of my heart there and took with me some of the light from the hearts that I had touched.

I will speak more of my travels to you, My Friend.

BUNDLE 10

THE FLOWERING STONE

My Friend who waits for me,

At long last, I stood near the lands of Condly. So light was my heart that I danced across the grassy plains from the Hunters' village. The Hunters had told me that from their village it was not far to Condly's. With quickened steps, the distance grew ever smaller.

I walked closer to Condly's home, then stopped for a short time to look at the ending place of my long journey. Here at last I stood, just before what I had wanted so long to see. Even from far off, I could tell that a village with great numbers of people were living there. Just beside it, a mountain stood high above the waters of the Lake with No End. Great, old trees stood under the mountain's shade. The houses I could see all stood under these trees with huge leaves, leaves that were like the ears of the animal with two tails. These houses were built in groups, forming circles, with an old tree in the center of each circle. Little Ones ran and danced from the bank of the great lake to the circles of houses. Grown Ones walked in the shade of the trees and the mountain, doing work of some kind, but with light steps. The wind was breathing constantly from the Lake, with a gentleness far softer than any breath of wind I had felt in our village under Tarantee.

As I walked closer still, I could hear sounds of laughter, of tree arms crackling in a fire, of work being done, and the whisper of the ever present waters of the Lake washing upon its bank.

I took a long breath, My Friend, before I walked into that village, what I thought was the end of my journey. As I entered the circle of circles, I saw Grown Ones with upturned faces all around me. The Little Ones played, dancing and singing around Old Ones who were sitting and talking in the shade of the trees within the circles of houses. Women carried bundles on their heads, singing as they walked from the banks of the Lake to their houses.

My thoughts told me that I should be able to see Condly's house, the home of the great queen, right away. Once again I saw her house in my thoughts. It was large, with many rooms and a roof that reached higher than the trees. The outside was colored like many of the feathered Ones and the flowers that grew along the path to my father's growing place, and Mutee's gift place. But this house, my eyes did not see as I approached the village. Was this Condly's home?

Many greeted me there as I walked into the village. Little Ones danced to my feet, and Grown and Old Ones came with outstretched arms and upturned faces.

150

"Hello, dear Traveler," said one man, light pouring from his eyes. An old woman hugged me as she spoke to me.

"You are welcome at our tables. What do your friends call you, my Child?"

"I am Caterin, of the village under the shade of Tarantee." At this, many of them laughed and put their hands together.

"Well, Caterin, I am Yongsee, son of Mutee," the man spoke again. "We have been waiting for you. My mother and the Visitors who traveled to Tarantee told us that your journey would lead you here to see Condly. Come. Come, and rest. Have something to drink." With that, Dear Friend, Yongsee led me with feathered hands to a place to sit under a great tree. The crowd followed, all dancing and laughing while the Little Ones sang. All were wanting to hear of the adventures of my journey. I wanted to see Condly, but I could tell that the hearts of these villagers were eager to greet me, so I took in some of their gifts from the earth.

As we rested in the shade, I told them the stories of my journey, from leaving the village under Tarantee so long ago, to my time with the Hunters. As I spoke, their faces lit with joy and they all nodded to each other. When I had finished, Yongsee spoke again in the growing darkness.

"Caterin, we thank you for telling us of your journey. It warms our hearts in the cold time to hear of such courage and light. Now you must close your eyes for this dark time. When the sun awakens again, I will take you to see Condly. She, too, has been waiting for you." Yongsee invited me into his small hut where a mat had been set for me. It was not long after I placed my head there that I closed my eyes.

I awoke before the sun did, while the darkness was beginning to fade to light. Yongsee was already sitting against a wall of his house, his face upturned, light shining from his eyes like a boy who had just named a fish in a stream.

"Caterin, you awake earlier than the sun! Here, have some gifts that I gathered from the tree friends of our village. When the sun rises over the mountain, I will take you to Condly." There have been many times that I have waited for the sun to rise, My Friend, but never have I watched and waited with my heart ready to burst with dancing than that sun time. Soon the time came.

"It is now for us to go to Condly," said Yongsee as he rose from the seat against the wall of his hut. He led the way out of his house, and we walked toward the foot of the mountain. "This is Parapet, our protector, and the One who brings us waters to drink." He pointed to the mountain as he spoke and kept walking slowly toward it. Ahead I saw several small huts just before a great cliff face. These huts too were in

152

a circle, and each was made of a circle, rather than the straight walls of the other houses in the village. In the center of this circle of houses stood an very old, bent tree. Yongsee led me past all of these to the small hut closest to the cliff. He stood for a moment outside it. "This is Condly's house. She welcomes you inside."

Was this the great queen's house? It looked very familiar, like Mutee's hut back in our village. It was much smaller than the house I had seen as Condly's in my thoughts. The roof was made from grasses. Arms and leaves of the Azule tree wound around to form one circular wall. Yongsee opened the door, and led me inside.

In the hut, sitting on a mat, was a small woman with two Visitors that I knew, sitting on either side of her. The room was full of light, but there were no openings to the outside, and no fire burning. So this was Condly, as Mutee had said, a very old woman. Her face and eyes looked as though the sun lived behind them. She had deep streams in her face which flowed with the same light. I looked down at her neck. She was wearing a neck ring of flowering stone. Just as with Mutee, the neck ring had become a part of her, but Condly's filled every part of her. Her hair, glowed as it streamed to the floor from her head, her hands shone as little suns, with beams of light stretching forth from her fingertips. She stood without effort to greet me.

"Caterin, I have long waited to hold you and look into the eyes of your heart. Come." She stood still, with her arms outstretched and her face upturned. I could not speak. Never before had my heart leapt like this.

I felt like a feathered One, my heart dancing in the air about the room, looping with joy. Condly walked slowly toward me, and took me into her arms. I felt as though hundreds of feathered Ones had just offered their softest clothing, warming me from the cold breath of the wind, and at the same time, cooling me from the heat of the high sun time.

With her touch, I felt like the sun's light had just slipped into my body, filling each part with its strength. She held me for a long time, saying nothing with her mouth, but everything with her heart. Then, she stood back a step from me, still glowing, still holding me with hands that were like the misted ones of my brother Dadock as I lay by the stream.

"Caterin, Mutee said that I would give you gifts, and so I shall. But, Caterin, you must know that I give you nothing that has not been with you all along, growing in your heart. I only stand to show you the gifts that have been yours. Come, let me show you."

Condly led me out the door of her hut. As we left, with the Visitors and Yongsee following, I saw that next to the mountain's cliff face, the waters had formed a very small lake just beyond Condly's hut. With one hand, she led me to this lake and asked me to bend over, to look into the Other World there.

As I did this, my thoughts could not catch up with my eyes. There in the waters of the Other World I stood, a Grown One now, rather than a Little One. Around my neck, instead of a vine with a feather, was a neck ring like Mutee's, Yongsee' s, and Condly's, shining with the light of the sun and the colors of the flowers. It's light spread outward, the glow filling my face and shoulders, almost down to my heart. I felt around my neck, but all my fingers touched was the feather.

"To you," Condly said, knowing the road my thoughts had taken. "This will always remain the feather that chose to lie close to your heart, unless you look to the other world such as this. Others will see what light shines from your heart as we see now. You are, Caterin, shining like the early sun already, for such a young one. But I knew, from what Mutee and my Friends, my Visitors, Arec and Tolemay, have told me that it would be so." She glanced at the two men that stood nearby with upturned faces. I looked again in the waters of the Other World, and still my thoughts and my eyes did not agree. My heart soared to the head of the mountain, over the Lake with No End, even back to Tarantee. Still, I had spoken no words to Condly.

"Great Queen, Condly," I finally was able to say. "Long have I waited for this time." As I spoke these words, Condly's eyes made a road of light to mine. She listened to my mouth, and the silent words of my heart. "My thoughts did not see you like this, but my heart dances as I look upon you now." I could say no more. Once more, she wrapped her arms around me, and thoughts of my mother holding me as a Little One, from long ago, returned. I stayed still, not wanting anything else. She held me for a long time. Finally, still holding me with one arm, Condly began walking with me, with the Visitors, and Yongsee, to the center of the village. As we walked, Condly talked with me.

"I have important things to do this morning, but I want you to stay by my side for many sun times, my Caterin. Say yes if your heart wants it so."

"Yes, yes, yes, Dear Queen!" I spoke with words that jumped from my heart. As we walked, Little Ones began to dance out of the houses that we passed. No words were spoken, but they followed us as we passed other houses. We walked to the bank of the Great Lake with No End, silently, Little Ones dancing behind us. When we reached the bank, the Little Ones all gathered close around Condly, some even touching her clothing.

"My Little Ones," she said, turning to face each one as she did. "The One whose life is in the light, the waters, the wind, the gifts of the earth, and your heart, never leaves you. Let your thoughts go now to where your heart lives, in the Heart of the One." As she finished saying this,

156

with a touch like the wind, she swung me around and began to dance. The Little Ones, too, danced and sang, there on the bank. Condly looked as though time was slipping from her body as she touched this Little One and another, and me, each one of us swinging round her with laughter. The Visitors and Yongsee danced and sang a song with Condly and the Little Ones that I had never heard before. I tell you now, Dear Friend, because I have learned this as a song upon my heart, singing it now each time the sun awakens.

> *Wake up, Dear Ones to light the way,*
> *And see and hear what One does say,*
> *Our times, our lives, live in One Heart.*
> *We dance, and laugh, and sing our parts.*
> *Wake up dear sun and wind, and waters too.*
> *And thank the One for what you do.*
> *We take, we give, in circles round,*
> *Our light, our life, in One are found.*

As we sang and danced on the bank, many of the Grown and Old Ones joined in. After a time, groups headed back to the village, or down to the bank of the lake. Condly led me to speak to each of the Little Ones, the Old Ones, and the Grown Ones. Then we too, headed back to the village.

"Caterin, my heart leaps and dances to see you with my eyes," Condly said. "Our village now shines with new light because of you." She led me back to her hut, where we took in gifts from the earth, and I told her the stories of my journey to her home.

Condly spoke with a voice like the warm wind. "It is time you heard the words of flowering stone that Mutee spoke of so long a time ago. These are words that you have grown in your heart already, as you could see in the waters of the Other World. But now I say these words from my mouth, so your thoughts too can now carry what your heart has held for so long.

"What is it you speak of, Condly?" I asked, looking into her heart through her lighted eyes.

"There is One, Caterin. This One is all. That power that gives the wind to the feathered Ones, lights our thoughts, and moves the fish in the streams, that power is from One, is One. There is no other power. I am only one voice for the One; as you are, Mutee is, your father. Feathered, furred, and green things growing and not, all are part of One from which they came. When you see this in your thoughts, in your heart, in your arms and legs, in all of you, there is only what we call joy. This is the secret that is not secret. Your parents know this with their hearts, but they have not seen it with their thoughts. Many see it one sun time or two within their thoughts. From one's heart to one's thoughts can be the longest journey."

"Is that what my child journey is?"

"Yes, Caterin, your thoughts rise with the sun. You have walked the journey from your thoughts to your heart. What do you find there?"

"Condly, my heart is full of laughter and dancing. I see a road of light between all things. But, dear Condly, what of Thretting? Does my father speak words that do not rise with the sun? Does Thretting live? Where is she? What does she do?"

"Good questions, my Caterin. I hope my thoughts can speak to yours, but even better, listen to the words of your heart as I speak. Dear Caterin, there is no Thretting who walks on the earth as I do. Thretting can only live in the dark thoughts of those who have not made the journey to the heart. Thretting's power is real when she is given life by those who see darkness in the light, but it is only for a time. Otherwise, she has no life of her own." Condly waved for me to follow her. We walked slowly out to the bank of the Great Lake with No End, and Condly spoke to me as her eyes looked upon the waters coming in and going out.

"I may be the Great Queen Condly, who you see before you, Caterin, but I have only the power that is the One's, none of my own. I am given this power for a time, just as those before me." She stopped and turned toward me, making a road between our hearts. "When it is my time to walk home into the earth, someone else will live as the Queen who speaks in this land for the One. That person must walk on the

159

earth, knowing the beasts and the Hunters, the mountains, the grasses, the furred and the feathered, all as living in the One, different petals of the same flowering stone, different beams of light from the same sun, different thoughts of the same One. That person will live with heart and thoughts that need no road between them, and with feathered hands and words that speak with light. This is a gift. It is also work, like what is done in the growing places. However, that which grows is not food for the body, but light and joy for the hearts of Little Ones, Grown Ones, and Old Ones. This is the work of all Mingdas, but my work, as those before me, and those after me, will be to stand as a road to One, to make the way easier for all."

"How can I become a Mingda?" I asked Condly, wondering if I would need to work in a growing place, or help in some way to become as Mutee and Mantoo.

Condly laughed with the smile of a Little One. "You became a Mingda in your heart the moment you came out of the earth from your mother. We all do. You walked each sun time as a Little One, and each sun time that you walked with Mutee, and each sun time of your child journey, opening as a flower to the Mingda you already were. But it is in this moment that your thoughts finally see who you are. It is in this moment that you are seeing Caterin as a Mingda. It is in this moment that you let go of thoughts of who you saw that was not Mingda, to walk as you truly are. It is in this moment that you are walking as a fully

160

opened blossom of flowering stone. From this moment on, you will only show more of your beauty to those who walk on the earth; you cannot become more of who you already are.

"A Pluma tree does not become more a Pluma tree once it has broken from the earth. It only shows more of its beauty. So it is with you."

After she spoke these words, I could say nothing. My thoughts stood silent as my heart danced within me. I looked at Condly again, seeing the light shining all around her and from within her. I wanted to be like her, to shine completely like the flowering stone that grew from around her neck the sun time before. I wanted to live as Mutee, walking my sun times with the Little Ones and the Old Ones. I wanted to see all the gifts from the earth and know that all are One by roads of light, heart to heart.

In that moment and at one time, Dear Friend, I saw this all in my thoughts and my heart. So began my time with Condly in the Village called Lumena.

I will speak more of my travels to you, My Friend.

BUNDLE 11

THE RING TAKES ME HOME

My Dear Friend who listens with a heart that speaks silently,

So it was in my first sun and dark time in the village with Condly. The next dark time, the feet of the villagers gave voice to our dancing hearts. We sang and danced as the darkness grew and the mist from the waters gathered around the mountain. It was long before anyone grew heavy and returned to their houses to rest. Even the Old and Little Ones joined us for most of that dark time. This was the way of those in the village to show me that they hold me in their hearts and in their thoughts. This was the one time that I was to wear the neck ring for all to see and share in joy.

As the fires leapt red and yellow in the center of the village circle, all danced around Condly, Yongsee, and me, singing as they did. The three of us made an inner circle, feathered hands holding together as we turned and turned. As we danced and sang, my feet were caught by a breath of wind. As I turned to look at Condly and Yongsee, the villagers dancing around us seemed to swirl into a mist before and below us, and we danced round and round, higher and higher.

Then I felt a breath of cool wind blow through my hair, and I stood alone before the house of Thar. I walked in, and saw that she and her husband and Little Ones were in their closed eye time. I tapped her on the shoulder.

"It is me, Caterin, Thar. I have come to tell you that I have seen Condly face to face. My heart runs with joy as the waters of a great stream. These words I wanted to tell you so that you could carry them in your heart as you walk to the growing places and play with your Little Ones." Thar looked up at me, her face showing fear of being hunted as I stood before her.

"Caterin, is it really you, or do my closed eye thoughts walk above me with such light?" I touched her hand, and her face upturned. "It is you! My heart sings to see you, Caterin."

"Look to your heart for the light that makes you sing, Thar. I must go now, but even so, I stay with you." Then another breath of the wind pulled me from her hut and into the gathered mists. Within another breath, I stood in the dark of the Great Family of Trees, and my friend the beast stood before me, taking in a creature that he had hunted moments ago. He stopped to look at me. Then he walked up to me and licked my feet with his rough tongue. I touched his head.

"I still hold you in my heart, you wondrous creature. May your hunting give you life for many cold and hot times to come. I will visit you often, each time I touch a furred or feathered

164

One." As I spoke, the wind breathed again, and I flew in the mist above the trees, like a feathered One looking down at the Great Family as I passed over it.

In those little moments, my thoughts did not wonder at this flight of my heart. And, just as I began to look to this, I saw the head of Tarantee in the distance, drawing ever nearer. Glancing below, I saw the Lake of Deep Waters and in the time it took to catch another breath, I was standing in the house of my father. He lay sleeping on his mat.

"Father, Caterin is here with you," I said with the voice of the wind as I touched his head. He sat up, and, with upturned face and eyes that shined, he returned my touch.

"Caterin! You have come back!"

"Yes, Father, I have completed my child journey. I have seen Condly face to face. I have held her feathered hands and danced with her. She is most beautiful to behold."

"Caterin, my heart leaps to see you. You are filled with light, my child. How can that be?"

"It is the light of the One, Father. It is the light that Condly holds, and Mutee holds, and Mantoo held. It is the light that you too, hold, if only your thoughts could look beyond the shadows to see what your heart holds. It is this light of yours that I can now see."

165

"Caterin, I must say words to you while you are here. When you left, I walked alone through the hot times and cold times. In those times that followed, I spoke often with Mutee. She told me of your walk through the Great Family, of your friend the Beast, and of your stay with the Hunters. My heart rested to hear that you were well. Now, she is helping me to prepare to walk alone again on my own child journey, to complete it. I, too, hope to see the face of Condly as you have, my Caterin. Mutee told me that you would walk into my house as you you do now, full of light. She also told me that you would not be able to stay now. This my thoughts and heart know. I will not hold you, but I hold the thought that I will see you and hold you again, dear Child."

With these words, my father stood up, and with upturned face that was filled with light, he reached out and held me close. "As I hold you now with my body, so too, will I hold you in my heart until I see you again."

"I, too, will hold you Father. My heart joins with yours in the light of this moment, to hold us together until we meet again in the village of Condly." As he let me go from his arms, the wind breathed again, lifting me through the top of my father's house to the hut of Mutee. She stood outside, looking up at the gathering mist as I floated into her feathered arms.

"Caterin, my heart told of your coming, and here you are." When Mutee said these words, Condly appeared with Yongsee. "Yongsee, my child. It is joy to see you again." Mutee wrapped her feathered arms around Yongsee as she spoke to him. I looked at them both, trying to hold the thought that Mutee had spoken. Then Yongsee turned to speak to me.

"Yes, Caterin, as I told you, I am Mutee's son. I did not go into the earth in the Great Family as many have thought. I made my child journey as you have done, and made my new home in the village of Condly. I have visited Mutee, my mother, many times as we do now."

"Why did you not tell the other villagers, Mutee?" I asked her.

"They who see darkness would not see the light of such visits, my dear Caterin. They would only see the shadow of Thretting and dark magic." The words she spoke rose with the sun of my heart, and I watched as their joy melted into one.

In the darkness in front of Mutee's hut, we formed a circle of light, glowing in the trees. "I can see that your heart has blossomed much since I placed the feather at your neck," Mutee said to me, her face streaming with light. Then she turned to Condly and Yongsee. "My heart flies in seeing you also, my friends. I know that you must return soon, but can I share a dance and a song with you?"

"Certainly, my dear Mutee." Condly took Mutee and Yongsee's hands and, forming a circle around me, began dancing in the light. Here is the song she sang, with Condly and Yongsee joining in.

> *Light to light our hearts do join,*
> *And feathered hands and feet do form,*
> *A circle round about the One,*
> *Whose light she sees with darkness gone.*
>
> *Light to light our hearts do fly,*
> *To see another and dance a while,*
> *We give, and live, and walk in One*
> *Whose light all creatures do come from.*
>
> *So, Caterin, we do join our hands,*
> *So sing with us, our merry band,*
> *And spin in light, as light we shine,*
> *And in One light our hearts do fly.*

Then I joined hands with their circle, dancing round and round. I closed my eyes and felt us all circling round. As I opened them again, I saw once more, the villagers of Condly's home gathered round our circle, dancing and laughing. Mutee, Yongsee, and Condly's rings and bodies shone, filling the circle of the village as with the sun's light.

Even the waters of the Lake with No End seemed to catch the light from our dancing and carry it far out into the darkness. When we had finished the dance, Mutee took me in her

168

feathered arms. Then she stepped back and held my hands.

"Caterin, I must return now to the village under Tarantee. Come see me often, and we will dance, sing, and talk together as we have this time. As I go, my heart joins with yours." As she said these words she melted into the lighted mist that gathered around us. I found my hands in the hands of Condly, my eyes looking into hers.

"Caterin, you have seen much this dark time that few hearts have eyes to see. Now it is time that you rest. When you open your eyes again, you will no longer be Child to anyone. You are now wholly Caterin, one who has seen the light of the One in Whom she walks. You will begin a new life in this light from this time forward."

I returned to Condly's hut and with few thoughts, closed my eyes. Throughout my closed eye time, again I saw my Father, and Mutee, Thar, and the Beast. I danced in a circle with my mother and with my brothers, Dadock and Deflic, laughing and singing songs of our hearts. When I awoke, Condly greeted me with streams of light from her upturned face.

In the early mist, as Condly, Yongsee, and I took in gifts from the trees of Parapet, Condly invited me to stay on with her. So I did, living in her hut, through the cold time and the next hot time. Many sun times did we walk together along the bank of the Great Lake with No End, among the villagers, and in the mountain. Even though

Condly was already an Old One, we became as sisters with the same heart.

In those sun times and dark times, my heart always danced, to songs that differed as the mists that gathered above. There were times there that I longed to share such music and dancing with Mutee, and my father. I knew that some time, I would return to Tarantee to live sun times and dark times with them, and so I have.

My Dear Friend,
As I finish in telling you of my child journey, I tell you also that you have a sister, a twin who lives in another land. There is much more I have told your twin, of the times between my first sun times with Condly, and my return at this time to the village under the shadow of Tarantee. Those words tell of the times under the shadow of Parapet and my journeys to other lands from the heart of Condly. Before she walked into the earth, Condly asked me to speak with your twin. So I did, leaving her within Parapet before returning here to Tarantee.

I speak with you now, My Friend, about my child journey, as thoughts in the warm light of my heart, once lived, twice held in my heart, third caught by your woody ears. I place these words, spoken to you, within your mother Tarantee. Some sun time, when you are ready, the light of the sun will invite you to blossom as a flower, sharing the beauty of these words with all who look upon it and listen to you. As you hold my words, so you hold the light of my heart.

170

My Friend, I will speak with you again.

Grace lay the last slat of wood down before her and looked around the cave at our group.

THE RING OF TRUTH

"That is all that is written here." She smiled broadly again. Dr. Sitzer looked up from the bundle that lay on the floor before them, breaking the silence.

"Quite a diary, isn't it? I'm beginning to wonder if this is an actual diary or just a myth written to teach the young people of the village. Parts of it seem a bit unrealistic, don't you think?" I could tell that he was posing the question to the group since his gaze passed around the room. However, he avoided looking at Grace, whose face was lighted by the equally unrealistic crystal neck ring. Just as he was posing this question, the wind blew again from deep within the cave and everyone's eyes riveted to Grace.

Her eyes grew wider as she raised her hands before her. The neck ring had been growing again, with the crystalline vines extending up into her face and down her arms, through her hands and all the way to the tips of her fingers. It appeared that light glowed softly from each of her fingertips, and a gentle ring of white light formed around her head as her face became more translucent, as though she had a gentle light shining beneath her skin.

"Oh, no!" I sighed. "It's starting again." I felt like I was the only one who could express

173

what everyone else was too shocked to say. "Grace, what is going on?" I looked her directly in the eyes, hoping that she had some explanation. What she said certainly gave an explanation, but not in the way that I expected or imagined.

"My Child, Grace, has offered to allow me to speak with you directly, and to you, my Little Ones." It was a voice, coming from Grace's lips, but with the quality of a very old person, and with a gentleness that melted my heart. "I am Caterin. You have listened to the story of my child journey, spoken through my wooden friend, and your friend, Grace. Many were my travels, and many were my sun times on this earth in what you call a body. Now, my spirit flies among the mountains, the lakes, and the trees as does the scent of the flowers and the breath of the wind.

What you have found here is not something new to you. It is simply a remembrance of who you are. I speak to you of what you call love. Do not let darkness shadow the joy of your hearts. In the sun times to come of this lifetime, you may each walk the journey to your heart as I did. Look beyond the shadow of the hole in your heart to the light of the One. Look to the light of the One to grow a flowering stone in your heart. Look to One light to give you the strength to reach your heart at the end of your child journey."

As soon as Grace spoke these last words, she folded her hands together, and bowed deeply before us. She stood straight and tall, took a deep breath, and slowly exhaled. A refreshingly cool breeze blew over us once again from behind her. As the wind blew, the vines of crystalline light in Grace's skin slowly dimmed and receded, first from her hands and fingers, then her face, slowly back to the neck ring itself. When the light had disappeared from Grace's body, she began to collapse toward the floor of the cave as if in slow motion.

I jumped forward and caught her. Dr. Sitzer, next to where she had stood, still sat dazed, dumbfounded. Sitting on the floor of the cave, I stroked Grace's head as I held her, calling to her over and over, hoping that she would awaken. Steve crouched down, gently lifted the ring from her neck, and placed it on the bundle of Paria leaves in front of her. Dr. Sitzer finally regained his some of his composure and grabbed a canteen of water, extending it to Grace.

"Here, Grace, take a drink." He said this with a gentle strength I had never heard from him. Still, she didn't move. The group gathered around her as she lay silent, eyes closed. She was breathing slowly and deeply.

"Check her pulse, Professor." Since he didn't seem to notice that she was still unconscious, I decided I needed to take charge. This jarred him from his trance enough to do what I asked.

175

"Slow but steady," he said looking up from his watch. "What have I done?" Dr. Sitzer said anxiously as Grace lay there, unmoving. "I shouldn't have continued with this whole thing. I should have known it would be dangerous to do this." A worried look grew in his face, and his voice trembled." A tear dropped from his cheek onto Grace's face as he crouched over her and murmured, "Please, please wake up Grace!" I felt a tremor roll through Grace's body. Then she opened her eyes, looking directly at Dr. Sitzer. She opened her eyes slowly, blinked at the Professor, and took another deep breath. In a long silence, she stared straight at him for a few long moments, then spoke softly, but with confidence.

"Grandfather, Daddy loves you. He knows you were just a kid when you left him. You didn't know what you were doing." She spilled the words quickly; her chest rising with emotions long held silent, she stopped a moment to take a breath. "He wants to see you again; Daddy, my father, he wants to see you, to talk with you, please!" I wondered whether she was delirious, or hallucinating. Dr. Sitzer must have been thinking the same thing, judging from what he said next.

"Grace, you're here with us, at Mt.Taree. Remember? I am Dr. Sitzer, and you're here with your archeology class." The Professor looked into her eyes, hoping for a sign that she would wake up completely. "You're not with your Grandfather. Remember me, Dr. Sitzer, your

176

archeology professor?" His face looked drawn and very worried as he repeated himself. "You are on an expedition, Grace. You fell and hurt your head. Wake up, please." His plea had a wisp of a cry in it.

"No, no, no," she said with quiet resolution. "I'm O.K." Grace raised herself on her elbows still staring with kindness at the Professor. "You don't understand. I'm fine. I feel better than I've ever felt. It's just that Caterin helped me find the way to my heart. Once I found my way there, I knew I had tell you now...I couldn't waste any more time...Grandfather...don't you see?" She took a deep breath again, all the while smiling wistfully at the Professor.

"Grandfather who?" I asked, hoping to draw her attention and shake off this dream. She glanced at me, searching my eyes, hoping I would understand, that someone would understand.

"Diana,...it's Dr. Sitzer...my grandfather. Caterin told me that my final healing waited here, that I must tell him now to close the hole in my heart. Caterin's ring, her love...it gave me the strength to say the words I've been wanting to say for years." She turned back to face the Professor again. "Daddy, er...my father...you know...Eric, your son...don't you remember? We both..." She gasped for air and fell back, her body weak, but the spirit in her eyes burning strong and bold, just as it was when she had grabbed the ring from the professor's hands the day before.

"What?" asked the professor. "What are you saying, Grace?" His eyes suddenly brimmed with tears when she mentioned the name Eric, then overflowed as the possibility that a granddaughter he didn't know existed lay on the floor of this cave, smiling brightly up at him. He stared away for a moment, tears rolling down his cheeks. "I lost track of Eric years ago...he was only eight...I acted so stupidly then." Shaking, a frail looking Professor reached for his handkerchief and turned as though to confess to us all. "I tried to find him once I came to my senses, but the adoption records had burned in a fire. I didn't think I'd ever see him..." He turned again to look at Grace, to tenderly take her young hand in his as he spoke again. "You're my...my...granddaughter, Grace? Is it really true?" She responded with a quiet smile, but the words she had long waited to say flooded the dim cave.

"Daddy talked about you all the time, as long as I can remember. He told me that he kept track of you ever since you left him. When I was old enough, we kept up with where you were and what you were doing. He's always been very proud of you, but he never wanted call you, to take the chance that you might not want to see him again. He lost you once; he couldn't bear to lose you a second time. I never had you to begin with, except through the pictures and articles we gathered. That's why I took all of your classes,

178

but without Caterin's help..." She paused slightly, and, with a twinkle of light in her eyes, she continued. "With what I know now, I think it's time we all came home. Please come with me to see him?"

Dr. Sitzer could speak no words in response, but sobbed heavily and said yes with every other part of his being. He enfolded Grace gently in his arms, as though she were a small child, and she held tightly to him. Rocking slowly in each other's arms, they cried and laughed together as we watched the flowers blossom in their hearts.

Caterin's Story - A Gift of Flowering Stone
Dan Erdman © 2014

Dan Erdman is a writer of fiction, non-fiction, song lyrics, and business training materials. He is also a musician/songwriter, having recorded the following tapes & CDs of his original compositions.

Power Within
God is Everywhere
On Strings of a Dove
Oasis

Another book by Dan Erdman:
Yoga & the 21st Century Man, Fitting Yoga in the Life of a Busy Man (with co-author Roger L. Null). Published 2007, Be You Productions, LLC.

Dan lives near Cincinnati, Ohio, and his home is his wife, Marcia. He has two adult daughters, Laura & Katie. Caterin's story was written as a bedtime story for Katie in the 1990's.

www.BeYouProductions.com